Sliding

Sliding

short stories
by
Leslie
Norris

Charles Scribner's Sons
New York

"A Big Night" was originally published in *Planet*.
"Snowdrops" first appeared in *The Shining Pyramid*.
The following stories appeared originally
in *The New Yorker:*
"Sliding", "Cocksfoot" and "Percy Colclough".
The following stories first appeared in
Atlantic Monthly: "Waxwings", "A House Divided",
"Three Shots for Charlie Betson",
"A Roman Spring" and "The Highland Boy".
"The Mallard" was first published in *Esquire*.
"Prey" was first published in *Audubon Magazine*.

Library of Congress Cataloging in Publication Data

Norris, Leslie, 1920–
Sliding : short stories.

CONTENTS: The waxwings.—Sliding.—Cocksfoot, crested
dog's-tail, sweet vernal grass. [etc.]
I. Title.
PZ4.N8562Sl3 [PR6027.O44] 823'.9'14 76-20503
ISBN 0-684-14775-0

1 3 5 7 9 11 13 15 17 19 V/C 20 18 16 14 12 10 8 6 4 2

Printed in the United States of America

Contents

Sliding

The Waxwings

Alwyn would have gone a fortnight ago, on his birthday, if he could have got away. All that day, despite the presents and the birthday cards and the afternoon party, he had been conscious of an enormous weightlessness behind his ribs, an almost irresistible awareness of freedom. On any other Saturday he would have gone, full pelt up the street, across the wide road where you had to be careful, then fast over the river bridge. He would have gone past Mr. Rampling's sawmills, past Mr. Rampling's house, which was the last house in town, past the laundry. Then the hills began. But that Saturday he was seven years old, and the petty responsibilities of his celebrations, the excitement of his little brothers, his friends visiting with parcels of toy boats and model aircraft, all had kept him firmly at home, locked in the center of the five short streets grown suddenly so irksome.

Then last Saturday his Uncle Ernie had come to see him. Uncle Ernie was so amusing, so inventive in his jokes, so daring in the games he improvised that the boy had no time to think of his escape. All afternoon he had played football in the garden, furiously and full of laughing, admiring his uncle's outrageous skill. After tea Uncle Ernie had drawn two dogs on a piece of cardboard and cut them out. One was Fred and one was Bert. He had been Bert, a black dog, and they had gone for a walk together all around the dining table. Fred, who was really Uncle Ernie, had said such mad and funny things that the game had to stop from time to

1

time for Alwyn to get his breath back. He wouldn't have wanted to get away last Saturday.

Once he had gone alone to the High Street, where he wasn't allowed on his own. This was because of the traffic and some other reason he couldn't remember. His mother had suddenly discovered that she had no milk in the house, and she had sent him to the Italian shop in the High Street. It had been a Sunday and everything was unnaturally still and quiet, the tall shops sleeping fast behind the fawn blinds that covered their windows. It had been a generous man in the Italian shop. He had dipped his gleaming scoop twice into an urn of milk, and then added an extra splash to the boy's white jug.

"That's a pint," he had said, "and a little drop more for you."

Every day the milk came to the house in pint bottles, early in the morning, and he had never carried it in a jug for such a long way before. It lurched and slopped up to the rim of the jug as if it had some malevolent life of its own, often leaping clear of the lip to spray itself in tiny, blue-white showers on the stones. The boy carried the jug very carefully in both hands, walking with small gliding steps so that the milk didn't have to jump up and down. George Evans saw him and jeered at him, so he put the jug down gingerly in a doorway and chased George Evans up the road, but he didn't catch him. The milk was quite safe when he got back to it, and he carried it home safely too. That was the farthest he had been on his own.

But today was different. He was walking calmly and deliberately up his street, and he was going to make it. He walked as quickly as he could without anybody noticing he was hurrying, and he was listening meticulously in case his mother should call him. Once he got as far as Mrs. Morgan's door he would not turn back whatever happened. His senses were screwed so tightly that his mother's voice, thin and distant, but unmistakably clear, sounded suddenly in the deepest coils of his ears. "Alwyn," it called; but it was only inside his head that made the sound. He looked back for a second. The front door of his house was blandly shut and his mother busy somewhere inside. Relieved, he lost his caution and ran.

He didn't stop until he was over the bridge and halfway down the fairground. It wasn't a proper fairground except for two weeks in the summer and at Christmas, and now it was quite empty except for some huge logs waiting to go to the sawmills. As he looked, the front gate of Mr. Rampling's garden opened, and a boy on a delivery bike wobbled out, kicking the gate shut behind him. It was Archie Baverstock, a big boy from school and a butcher's boy on Saturdays. Archie's face was round and serious, and he wore a striped apron. He looked down from his bike at Alwyn.

"Hello, young 'un," he said tolerantly. "You're out of bounds, aren't you?"

The boy felt an immense gratitude to Archie. He had never heard anything so precise and evocative in his life before, and he grinned his delight at the older boy. "Yes, I am, Archie," he called, "I'm out of bounds."

But Archie did not turn his head. Moving with slow, unthinking circles of his legs, his heels on the pedals, his toes turned out, he entered cautiously into the stream of traffic on the road at the end of the fairground.

Alwyn hurried on toward the sawmills. He could hear already the petulant rasp of the saw as it ate into the wood, he could smell the moist, absorbent scent of the sawdust as it whirled in smoky falls from the whining teeth. There would be sawdust everywhere, on the ledges, whitening the forearms and eyebrows of the sawyers, in drifts on the ground, with wet brown patches underneath leaking places in the roof. It was fine in the sawmills, but he wasn't going there. He stopped only to drink from the brass tap that stood on a long pipe coming straight out of the ground. On a journey as long as his might be, you never knew where the next drink was coming from.

Once past the laundry he was on the narrow road, just

wide enough for one vehicle, that led up into the hills. He looked at it speculatively. Up to now it had been remembered ground, but from here on it would be all exploration. He took a deep breath and went for the hills.

For perhaps a mile it was gentle gradient, cutting into the side of the mountain and running south, climbing so imperceptibly that the boy was astonished to see the roofs of the town unfold themselves below him. He saw Mr. Rampling's house as finely detailed as a doll's, he saw the long gray roof of the laundry with little jets of steam pulsing out of its pipes, and far away he could see, he thought, the roofs of his own street. But he wasn't sure. The town lay flat and strange under his eyes.

Then he turned into the steep of the track, leading to a thin mist of wood high up, and beyond that, the bare ridge of the summit at which he was aimed. He climbed now with a steady certainty, feeling his legs push away at the gravel, his lungs laboring a little. Here and there paths led off to the small hill farms, their houses painted white, their suspicious collies barking as he passed the gates.

A stream was running alongside the road now, a narrow stream with occasional music only, too swift and shallow for fish. But as he met the small shrubs at the entrance to the wood, the water had filled enough of a depression to make a pool. A young man squatted near the pool, on his hunkers, as colliers sat. His suit was blue and shiny, and his cap lay on the grass at his side. Standing up to its hocks in the water was a brindle greyhound, so still that its reflection shivered only in the moving water. Alwyn was as unmoving as the dog, but the young man knew he was there.

"This stream, now," he said. "Did you know it has some remarkable qualities?"

Alwyn walked over and sat near the young man.

"No," he said. "What do you mean, remarkable qualities?"

The young man looked at him thoughtfully.

"It heals," he said. "If, for example, you had sprained

your ankle—although that would be unlikely for someone as young and limber as you are—but if you had, all you would need to do is to hold your feet in the curative waters of this pool."

"Is that what your dog is doing?" asked Alwyn.

The young man nodded.

"Goliath," he said, "is suffering from a slight muscular strain, or perhaps he has injured a fetlock. Whatever it is, you may be sure that he is cured now. You might care to put that to the test. Here is Goliath's lead—we'll fasten it to his collar, thus, and you will take him at a fast trot up the road until you hear me whistle. Observe the perfection of his action, and only half an hour ago I had almost to carry him here."

Alwyn arose at once. An opportunity to take this marvellous silent dog for a walk was not one to throw away. He took the leather strip and trotted up the lane. Docile and graceful, the long dog went with him. He was not a bit lame, and when they were whistled back Alwyn wheeled around in his tracks and Goliath paced elegantly with him.

The young man was stretched comfortably, about to light a cigarette. He told Alwyn that his name was Terence O'Neil, and that Goliath was his father's dog.

"If it were my dog," he said, waving his cigarette expansively, "I should give him at once to you, because I have never seen so immediate an affinity between boy and dog. And Goliath is not a dog who gives his affection lightly, no, anything but."

Alwyn looked at Goliath. To own this dog would be an unthinkable honor. He sighed.

"In any case," he said, "I shouldn't think my parents would let me keep him."

Terence nodded with understanding.

"I'll tell you what," he said, "I'll let you take him again, exactly as you did last time. I wouldn't let anyone else do this, since exercising a greyhound is a very exacting business. Go more slowly this time."

And he took out a newspaper from his pocket, a pencil from another, and began to underline certain names of horses on the racing page. He was generous enough to allow Alwyn to take Goliath for several more walks, but at last, after a quick glance at his watch, he thanked Alwyn with ceremony, took the lead, and walked rapidly away. The boy watched him go, and then he turned uphill.

Now he was in the thin cover of the hawthorn wood, the dark red berries shining like beads on the short, leafless trees. It was much steeper too, and occasionally he pushed with his hands on his thighs, to help him climb. He couldn't see the top of the mountain any longer, but he knew that once clear of the trees, the bare line of the summit would not be far away.

Then the birds came. Ripping in hundreds through the dry twigs of the hawthorns, they tore and devoured the scarlet berries with ferocious, brittle energy. They were so brilliant that the boy cried his delight aloud, holding out his arms to them. Their voices were weak and high, whispering and trilling unceasingly as they flew, but their colors, oh, the colors. Their heads held crests of chestnut, a black stripe ran dramatically through each eye, their bodies were tinged with pink, the incredible tails, short and thick, were tipped with a band of yellow as bright as summer. But it was their wings, carrying them boldly through the trees as they ate like locusts, that the boy saw most clearly. Strongly barred with black and white, the secondary feathers looked dipped in vermilion sealing wax, as hard and shining as sealing wax. He thought they were like hundreds of candles sparkling through the trees. First there were a few birds, then a flying cloud of them going through for as long as a minute, then the stragglers, at last only the echo of their thin, persistent voices. Alwyn turned to watch them vanish through the wood, his eye led down the path and on to the town lying still and far under him.

He knew it was time to return. Nothing left on the mountain could equal that visitation of the waxwings, the glittering birds that had flown from Scandinavia, from the cold hunger of Russia. They had flown in their packs over the snow-pocked rollers of the North Sea almost into his fingers, and they blazed in his illuminated mind as he jogged downhill through the dying afternoon.

He saw the chimneys of the town begin to push the heavy smoke into the sky as people warmed their houses for the evening. It was late. He wondered if there had been a search party out for him. He was very hungry.

Turning into his own street, he slowed to an aching walk. His mother was outside the house, waiting for him. She was angry, and her voice was high and shrill. He stayed some distance away, watching her, measuring the extent of her anger.

"Where have you been?" she called. "What have you been doing?"

Already a quick relief was replacing her temper. She had watched for some time his growing independence and had half expected something like this, some exploration into his own identity. Now she saw with compassion the small boy standing before her, his face bewildered and frustrated by his inability to express the significance of his journey, the marvellous vision of the waxwings. She saw the puzzled tears form in his eyes.

"Oh, Mam," he said, "my boots is hurting."

She put her arm around his shoulders, and smiling, led him indoors.

Sliding

The cold had begun very suddenly on Tuesday night, when Bernard had gone out to play. The boys were playing kick-the-tin in the lamplight at the top of the street, and nobody realized how cold it was until Randall Jenkins went home for his cap and scarf. Then they all felt the bitter weather—at their knees, their wrists, the tips of their ears. Bernard went indoors and borrowed his father's knitted scarf and found his own old gloves from last winter. Pretty soon, the game was on again and they forgot about the weather.

That night in bed, the sheets were hard and slippery, unfriendly as ice. Carefully, by an act of will, Bernard made warm a place in bed exactly the same shape as his body, thin and hunched under the covers. He extended it gradually, inch by inch, sending his toes gently into the cold until at last he was straight and comfortable. Everything was fine then, except that he had to pull the blankets firmly about his ears and shoulders. In the morning, the window was covered with frost flowers, and the kitchen fire blazed ferociously against the Welsh winter. He called for Danny Kenyon, as usual, on the way to school. Danny was his best friend, and they ran all the way, although Danny was short and plump.

Bernard was used now to the ice. Out in the yard, the tap had been frozen for days and a tongue of glass poked out of its mouth. Every morning was gray and spiteful, churlish light making the whole world dingy. Patches of hard grit gathered in the gutters and at the corners of streets, whipping against the boy's face and into his eyes. All day long, the shops kept their lights on, but there was nothing cheerful about them; only Mr. Toomey's shop was strong with color, because of the brilliant globes of his pyramids of oranges.

In school on Friday morning, Albert Evans began to cry. The teacher asked him why, but Albert wouldn't answer. It was Randall Jenkins who told about Albert's legs. The inside of his thighs was chafed raw—red all the way from his groin to his knees. The skin was hard and angry, and there were weeping cracks in it. The teacher let Albert sit in front, near the stove, and he didn't have to do any arithmetic. When Bernard told his mother about Albert's legs, she narrowed her mouth and said that Annie Evans had no more sense than the day she was born, and then she took a pot of ointment over to Albert's house. While she was out, Bernard's father told him it had been the coldest day in more than twenty years. It was funny about skin and cold weather. Some boys turned red because of the cold, and some rather blue, and Danny Kenyon's knees went a kind of mottled color—but he only laughed. When Bernard's mother came back, she was vexed. "Poor little scamp," she said. "It's agony for him to walk at all."

After breakfast on Saturday morning, Bernard climbed into his den, which was the room above the stable in the yard. His father had whitewashed the walls for him, and together they'd carried up some old chairs from the house. Two large kitchen tables, covered with paints and bits of models and old newspapers, stood side by side under the windows. His record-player was there, too, and it was warm because of the oilstove. It was a fine room, with an enormous spider in the corner of the roof and a web thick and black against the white wall. Bernard sat in a chair near the stove and began to think of the things he would do when the summer came and he would be nine, going on ten. He and Danny Kenyon would go camping, they would find a field that nobody else knew about, and every day would be cloudless. He made the field in his head—the perfect green of its grass, its great protective tree in one corner, and its stream so pure that you could see every fragmentary pebble, every waving strand of weed in its bed. They were too young to go camping. He knew that.

And then Randall Jenkins climbed the stairs. He was grinning. He carried about his neck a pair of heavy boots, tied by their laces. He took them off and dropped them proudly on the floor, where they stood bluntly on their uncouth soles, exactly as if they still had someone's feet in them and invisible legs climbing up from them. Randall held out his hands to the stove and danced slowly around it, revolving so that he warmed himself all over.

"Coming sliding?" he said. "This afternoon? We're all going—on the big pond; it's holding."

"I'll ask," said Bernard. "I expect it will be all right."

He thought of the big pond under the hills, its heavy acres hundreds of yards wide, the water cold and thick. It held in its silence fabulous pike, more than a yard long and twenty pounds in weight, although Bernard had never seen one. He didn't like the big pond.

"You'll need special boots," said Randall. "I've borrowed my brother's—take a look at them."

He lifted the great boots and held them for Bernard's inspection. The soles were an inch thick and covered with a symmetrical pattern of bold nails—flat squares shining like silver. Crescents of smooth metal were screwed at heel and toe into the leather, the edges worn thin as a razor.

Randall rubbed his sleeve over the scarred toe caps, breathing on them as he burnished.

"These are the ones," he said. "My brother's old working boots. They might have been made for sliding."

"They're too big for you," said Bernard.

"Size 7," said Randall with satisfaction. "My brother's grown out of them. Three or four pairs of socks and they'll fit me—you watch, I'll scream right across the pond."

He moved the boots through the air as if they were fighter planes.

"You'll need a pair like this," he said. "Otherwise you'll never go any distance."

Randall was lucky to have big brothers. Bernard thought dismally of his own boots—light, gentlemanly, with rubber soles and heels. His grandfather didn't like rubber soles and heels, either. Only thieves and policemen, he had said, two classes of society with much in common, wear rubber on their feet. Bernard didn't understand that.

"Is Danny Kenyon coming?" Bernard asked.

"Sure," Randall said. "We're all going. I told you."

After lunch, they all went to the pond, protected by layers of clothing against the wind's knives, their woollen hats pulled over their ears. Some of the boys had managed to borrow heavy boots, just to be like Randall Jenkins, and they clumped awkwardly up the hill as they learned to manage their erratic feet. Randall Jenkins turned out his toes, shuffling around corners like Charlie Chaplin, and they all laughed.

Bernard began to feel very happy. He began to imagine the long quietness of his gliding over the ice. He thought of thick ice, clear as glass, beneath which the cold fish swam, staring up with their goggle eyes at the sliding boys. He thought of ice like a dazzling mirror set in the hills, on which they could skim above their own images, each brilliant slider like two perfect boys—one upside down—joined at the feet. In his happiness he jostled and bumped against Danny Kenyon, and Danny charged right back at him, until they were both laughing and the wind blew away their white breath in clouds from their mouths.

But the pond was a disappointment. Winter had taken all the life from the hills, and the face of the ice was gray and blind—the color of the flat sky above it. There were no reeds at the lake's edge. Featureless, the ice stretched on, swept by an unhindered wind. The boys bent their heads down against the brutal cold. Their voices were feeble; they felt small and helpless. Only Randall Jenkins was unaffected. Whooping and waving at the ice, he began to run, lifting his enormous boots in slow, high-stepping strides. He ran on, planting his laughable feet one after the other so heavily that Bernard imagined he could hear the whole bowl ringing; and then, his legs rigid, both arms raised for balance, he slid with comic dignity. They all rushed after him, sliding and calling. The afternoon was suddenly warm and vigorous.

Bernard was a good runner, and he hurled himself along so that the momentum of his first slide would be memorable. He raced past two or three of the boys and then stopped, his legs braced wide, head up, arms raised. He was expecting something birdlike, something approaching flight, but nothing happened. His rubber soles clung wickedly to the surface of the ice and he slid no more than a few yards. He was inconsolable.

He shuffled cautiously along the margins of the ice, tentative and humble. Far out, in the wide middle of the pond, he could see the dark figures of his friends, freely sliding, gyrating, crouching, skating on one leg. Their voices came bouncing to him high and clear like the calling of seagulls. But he ran alone at the edge of the lake, unable to slide. Then, unexpectedly, without warning, he found himself free of the binding friction that had held him. He had begun to glide. He sat on the bank, lifted one foot, and inspected the sole of his boot. A thin layer of polished ice, thinner than a postage stamp, had built itself onto the black rubber. He saw that the other boot was also transformed, and he ran jubilantly into the heart of the pond, far outstripping the loud boys, sliding far and fast, hearing their admiration and surprise. The pond was his.

Late in the afternoon came two young men, tall, with deep voices, all of seventeen years old. They strapped on their

sharp and proper skates, and skated expertly. Briefly, the
boys watched them, but soon Randall Jenkins had organized a game of follow-my-leader. Randall was a superb
leader, his invention and audacity encouraging them to a
skill and daring they had not known they possessed. The
last dare was to run as fast as they could toward the ice from
the shore itself, leaping from the bank at full speed. Randall
raced forward, his long slow legs gathering pace as he ran,
and then he leaped high outward from the bank, landing
yards out. Rigid as a scarecrow, he sped on, stopping at last
a prodigious way out, and standing absolutely still in the
attitude of his sliding. One by one they followed him, although nobody was as brave as Randall, nobody would hurl
himself as uninhibitedly from the steep bank. At last, only
three boys were left. Bernard thought he had never seen
anything as lovely as the dark ice, hardly lit at all as the
light faded, and the still figures of his friends dotted about
on it, not moving, their arms in a variety of postures, their
bodies bent or upright. He took a great breath, and ran. He
had never felt so light, he was full of fiery energy. He
reached the bank and thrust himself so urgently, so powerfully, that the exhilaration of his leap made him gasp. He
hit the ice beautifully, and felt at once the speed of his sliding, and he knew that nobody had ever slid so far. Stopping
at last, he looked around. He was yards farther than Randall
Jenkins, miles farther than the other boys. Jackie Phelps
was slowing miserably a long way off, and only Danny was
left to jump.

He could see Danny up on the bank, preparing to run,
swaying from one foot to the other, bent forward at the
waist. Cupping his hands, Bernard shouted, "You'll never
reach me!"

Danny waved furiously. You could see that he was going
to give it all he had by the way he set his shoulders. He ran
forward and leaped wildly from the bank. Bernard could see
him so clearly that everything seemed to happen in slow
motion. He saw Danny hit the ice and knew that it was
wrong. Danny landed on his heels, not on the flat of his

feet, and his body was already tilting gently backward. He sped along, the slope of his body already irrevocably past the point of recovery. They saw his heels leave the ice, and for a perceptible moment he sailed through the unsupporting air before the back of his head cracked frighteningly against the surface. He lay broken and huddled. Bernard could not move. He could see Danny in a black heap, but he couldn't move toward him. It was Randall Jenkins who reached him first, and they all ran in behind him.

They crowded around Danny, looking down at him. His face was still and white, his eyes closed. As they looked, a little worm of blood appeared at one nostril and curled onto Danny's lip. What if he should die? Bernard bent, and in an urgency of terror lifted his friend. Randall helped him, and together they hauled Danny to the bank. Some of the boys were crying, and Randall set them to collect twigs, pieces of paper—anything that would burn. Bernard took off Danny's gloves and rubbed his hands in his own. Danny's fingers were very cold, but in a while he began to move and groan. Twice he opened his eyes, without recognizing them and without saying anything. Randall lit a fire, and it burned with a dull light, sullenly. He sent all the boys except Bernard to find more fuel, told them to rip branches from small trees. Bernard wiped the blood from Danny's nose, and after a while the bleeding stopped. It hadn't been very much, he comforted himself. His knees hurt from bending down so long. Behind him, Randall had whipped the fire into a huge blaze that pushed away the darkness, and the boys sat near it, not speaking. Danny moved heavily, sat up, and looked at Bernard.

"Oh, my God," said Danny Kenyon. "What happened?"

He was all right; everything was all right. The boys cheered, slapped each other on the back, put Danny to sit even nearer the fire. They danced and sang, released from fright, and they were pert and arrogant when one of the young men suddenly appeared.

"What's the matter with him?" he asked, bending over Danny.

"Nothing," said Randall airily. "Nothing at all."

"None of your business," said Jackie Phelps, out of the darkness.

"How old are you?" said the young man to Bernard.

"Ten," lied Bernard. He pointed to Randall. "And he's eleven," he said.

"Get that boy home," said the young man. "How do you feel, son?"

"Great," said Danny. "I feel great."

"Get home," said the young man. "And the rest of you see that this fire is out."

He skated into the darkness. Bernard could feel the iron shearing of his blades.

The fire was very hot. Bernard could imagine it warming a thin crust of frozen soil, then maybe deeper, a half inch deep. Already he could hear the ice hiss in the released ground. He sat with his back up against Danny's back, so they were both comfortable. All the boys sat around. They were very quiet.

Bit by bit, the dark and the cold crept into the interstices of the flames, winning the night back for winter. Randall got up and stamped about. His feet had gone to sleep.

"Time to go, lads," he said. "Time to go."

They stood up and followed obediently behind Randall. Bernard was so tired that his legs were slow and stiff, and his mind was always about two steps in front of them, but in a little while they got better. The boys went down the lane past the old rectory and started down the hill toward the town. A night wind flew at them as if it cared nothing for people and meant to blow straight through them. Bernard began to shiver. What if Danny had died? He saw again Danny's face as he lay on the ice, as white and stiff as a candle. As he looked, an imaginary worm of blood crawled from Danny's nose and covered the side of his cheek. He closed his mind from the terror of it and put his arm over Danny's shoulder.

"How do you feel?" he whispered, but Randall heard him.

"He feels great," Randall Jenkins roared, his voice red as fire. "What's the matter with you? He feels fine!"

"I'm O.K." said Danny. "Honest, I'm O.K."

A few small flakes of snow fell out of the sky. The boys felt them hit their faces, light as cobwebs, and then vanish. It was intolerably dark and cold. As they entered the first streets of the town, the boys moved together for solace and started to run. They trotted close together, moving home as one boy through the darkness, united against whatever terror might threaten them.

Cocksfoot, Crested Dog's-Tail, Sweet Vernal Grass

The year I was thirteen, my father died. He died in the middle of July, and he was buried on a Wednesday, in the cemetery at the edge of town, on a hot day. Up there on the low hill, a trace of breeze was welcome. I was in my mourning suit, buttoned to attention, and the lightness of moving air was scarcely perceptible on my face. We stood unmoving at the side of the raw grave, the preacher's voice dry as a rasp of grasshoppers. My uncle, down from Northampton, stood next to me. I had been named for him: Frederick. We were both Frederick Galloway. That morning, he had put his hand on my shoulder, but I had moved away. I'd done my crying. Now I watched the heads of seeding grasses on the neighboring boundaries of the cemetery as if they alone were real. They moved delicately and aimlessly in the tiny wind, obeying rules of an excellent sort. When the service ended and the men of the family and their friends began to talk again, breathing vigorously in an attempt to become immediately normal, I let them go. I watched them move down the hot paths toward the gate where the cars were waiting for them, and then I stepped among the tall grasses, looking at them, staying with them. I was there a long time.

Boys of that age are the world's experts. Driven, perhaps, by a new need to understand at least something of an increasingly perplexing world, they choose some part of it—pigeons, motorcycles, the activities of pop stars or footballers—and this they study with an absorbed energy, knowing everything. With me, it became grasses. When I got to bed that night, I still saw clearly the dipping heads of grass, heard the harsh stalks rustling together in the heat.

That summer, I read all I could find about grasses. Even now, I can remember their names: perennial rye grass, timothy, meadow foxtail, quaking grass, erect brome (with beautiful purple heads), sheep's fescue and red fescue, cocksfoot, crested dog's-tail, sweet vernal grass.

We lived in a South Coast town, small, tightly knit, very provincial. A slow river ran past the edge of the town and through an untidy marsh into the sea. In the spring of the year, I had been walking on the salt flats, through muddy rivulets, looking for ducks' nests. Few people ever went there, but I was there often. In winter, it was marvellously wild and solitary, although it couldn't have been more than a dozen acres altogether.

That spring day, before my father died, I met Edgar Martin down on the marsh. He was a big, awkward boy, a class above me at school, but we'd never spoken before. He had three eels in his hand, and he held them up in quiet triumph. Gray and shining, they hung easily in his grip, as if they were relaxed, as if they were going along with him willingly, trustingly. One of them was the biggest eel I'd ever seen. We became friends, Edgar Martin and I.

I used to spend a lot of time that year up at the Martins' farm, north of the town, and as the year grew warmer we swam most afternoons in the river pool at the bottom of the big meadow. It was a perfect pool. The river had cut deeply into the mild soil until it reached stone, and now it rested, four or five feet deep, on a long slab of rock. If you dived underwater, you could see the stone, layered and flat, tilted slightly, and carved by the melodious filing of water. It looked dark green in color, but if you brought out a loose, flat stone, it dried gray, with darker streaks running through. I didn't like that. I threw every dry stone lying about the pool back into the water. I used to do this after I'd had my swim, marching up and down, reclaiming stone after stone for the river. Edgar Martin used to laugh at me.

One hot afternoon, I walked down to the pool. Edgar was already in, floating on his back and churning the water with his feet into a small foam. I'd been to the hospital to see my father, and it hadn't been interesting. He was asleep, and I sat there, close to the white metal bed, for thirty minutes. We never spoke much, my father and I, but it was better when he was awake. He would say some quite funny things then, clearing his throat first so that his quiet voice would have a better chance of being heard. That afternoon the nurse told me that I could leave, since it seemed unlikely that he would wake up, and I walked up the hill through the streets until I came to Edgar's farm.

I was glad of the sweet water. I let myself loll through it as if I were as boneless as waterweed, drifting from the head of the pool along its slow-moving currents, then swimming back and floating again, over and over. The whole afternoon slept in the heat.

It was a sharp call from Edgar that aroused me. I turned to see a snake swimming toward me, its head two or three inches out of the water, like a periscope. I couldn't see its body, but some movement of the surface, or perhaps a minute swaying of its head and neck, suggested its wriggling length. I saw all this with perfect clarity, and the next second I was out of the water and crouched on the riverbank. I don't know how I did this; it was a kind of effort I had never made before. Edgar began to laugh, but I could see he'd been impressed.

"Boy," he said, "you can go like a bloody fish when you've a mind to!"

We dressed slowly and lay on the grass to wait for the cool evening.

"That's the cemetery up there," said Edgar, "that's the back of it. The council wants to buy the next field so they can make the cemetery bigger, but the man who owns it won't sell."

"I know," I said.

I turned on my side to look, spitting out a sweet white stalk of grass as I did so. The cemetery stood on its little hill, and the heat wavered all the outlines between, so that the hill danced on shifting air and nothing was real.

"It was only a grass snake," Edgar said when we got up to go. "Quite harmless."

"I know," I said.

We walked through the farmyard, and Edgar's mother asked me to stay to supper, so I did.

The next day, my father died. It was a Sunday.

My mother and father were both North Country people, she from Hull, and he from the North Riding of Yorkshire. They had travelled south immediately after their marriage, knowing there was little chance of work in the North. At first, they had thought themselves fortunate, but as time went by they realized that their successes would be small and ordinary. My father found work almost at once as a booking clerk on the railway. He was a small, dapper man, quiet and droll in speech. He seemed amused by everything he saw; he wore his mouth always in a gentle smile.

They worked long hours in those days before the war. When I was small, I used to lie awake in the little room above the front hall until I heard the sound of my father's cane tapping against the pavement as he walked toward the house. He would open the door so quietly that often I wouldn't hear him enter. I wouldn't know he was home until I heard his light cough. I'd go to sleep then. He always carried a cane. It was an affectation that annoyed my mother. She thought he was making himself old before his time, but when she said this he would only smile.

When I was older, I sometimes spent a winter evening sitting with my father down at the railway station, in the booking office. He had a large fire there, always, but it was still unbearably cold. I'd sit by the fire until I saw my father begin to fidget. He was afraid that the stationmaster, silly, self-important Billy Fletcher, would come in and catch me sitting there. I was not afraid of Billy Fletcher. His two sons, Sam and Edwin, were in school with me—round, timid boys who turned their heads away when I looked at them. I used to threaten them and beat them up sometimes, because my father was afraid of the stationmaster.

Some time after my father died, I went down to the station. It was in the early winter, in November. There were only two platforms. From one the trains moved eastward along the coast before turning inland for London, and from the other the slow files of carriages moved once an hour down into Hampshire and Dorset. In those days, I knew the times of all the trains. The platforms were lit by gas lamps overhead, each light formed of three frail gas mantles like buds of stiff lace set in a triangle under a glass dome. They threw irregular circles of weak, yellow light on the wooden planks. Bleak, unexpected winds searched the corners of the station buildings, and if you stood under one of those gas lamps, the night seemed to hiss and pop as small flames puffed in the gusts. It was as desolate and sad a place as I've ever stood in.

My father was never promoted. He just moved slowly through his life, a thin, slow booking clerk, getting thinner and slower.

I'd always been pretty good at school—not marvellous, but good. That year, somehow, everything went wrong, and I began to let things slide a little. I used to stay away two or three afternoons every week, and I'd walk through the fields, not thinking very much about anything. That was the time I learned about grasses. I watched them grow heavy-headed with seed, I watched them yellow and die, I saw them become spent bents and tussocks flattening under winter.

My Christmas report from school was bad, and my mother was more angry than I'd seen her before. She had a thin Northern face, and her voice had got into the habit of complaining. From then on, we seemed to be enemies, and I spent very little time in the house. One day at school, old Hughes, who taught English, spoke to me.

"Your work," he said, "your work is so bad now. What are you going to do?"

"I don't know, sir," I said.

"You can't go on like this," he said, very kindly. I could see he was worried.

"No, sir," I said. At that moment, I was determined to work immensely hard, to astonish everyone by my industry and progress.

"Now, look," said old Hughes, "it seems to me that you have very little interest at all in your work here. You're fourteen now—it might be better if you were to leave school and get yourself a job. What does your father want you to do?"

I looked up at him savagely.

"I haven't got a father," I said roughly.

He was bewildered and dismayed, and I was merciless. He had no right to live in a comfortable world where the death of my father was unknown.

"He's dead," I said. "He died last July."

Old Hughes' face was red and stupid.

"All the more reason, then, for you to work hard, either in school or out of school, wherever you decide," he said.

That night I had another fierce row with my mother. I remember that the skin of her thin neck was blotched with anger and that she was shaking with temper. And I remember what she said as I left the house: "You're like your father. He never fought and you'll never fight. You'll go down as he went down."

My little sister, six years old, began to cry.

The next day, I looked for old Hughes at school, and told him I would be leaving at the end of term.

"Fine," he said. "Come and see me before you go."

I nodded, but we both knew it would never happen. We'd said our piece.

It was time to leave. I knew that. I wasn't really like my father. My hands and feet were much bigger than his. I walked differently, more heavily; my features were larger and coarser. I looked older than fourteen.

I was an embarrassment to my mother, who hoped, I knew, to marry again. One day I found that she had cleared out everything that had been my father's, giving things away, burning things in the garden. I rescued his razor and brushes from the bonfire and kept them in the garden shed. They were in a small leather case—a safety razor and two Bakelite tubes for the brushes. She didn't know I had them. After the bonfire, she looked a lot happier and began to sing about the house. I think she was seeing one or two men. She was only thirty-five.

One Saturday morning before the end of term, I walked down to the station to see old Billy Fletcher. He was standing outside his office, encased in officialdom, his uniform tight, his peaked hat brave with braid. I asked him if I could speak to him. I was taller than Billy Fletcher, despite his proud hat.

"Of course, my boy," he said. "Any time, any time. Come in, come in."

We went into his office. From his windows you could see a long way down the track. A mile along the narrowing line, I could see the signal box, and I wondered which of my father's friends was on duty there. I sat on the edge of a chair and let Billy Fletcher talk.

"We miss your father here," he said, "yes, we miss him. A real gentleman, and there aren't too many of them about. A sad loss, and so young, too. Well, there it is."

He blew sadly and complacently down the swell of his plump vest and asked what he could do to help me.

"I'm leaving school in just over two weeks, and I'll need a job," I said. "I was wondering . . ."

He shook his head and let his eyes look importantly at nothing.

"There's nothing," he said at last. "No, nothing at all. The company would like to help, but we're full staffed. It would be different now if you were prepared to leave home."

"I can leave home," I said quickly. "I'd prefer to leave home."

Mr. Fletcher opened his eyes in surprise and smiled with baffled content.

"You boys," he said. "You youngsters! You'll try anything. My two are just the same. Try anything!"

I thought of Sam and Edwin Fletcher, those soft, cowering boys, and sneered in my head.

"Come in next week," said Billy Fletcher. "I'll be in touch with Head Office on Monday, and we'll hope to have good news for you."

He was as good as his word. On the following Tuesday, I had a letter offering me a post as parcels clerk in Swindon, to start immediately I left school.

I left home on a Sunday evening in April. As I carried my case down the street, I saw my sister playing with five or six other little girls. They were skipping, using a long rope, two of them turning the ends while the rest hopped seriously inside the whirling rope, each with her hands on the shoulders of the child in front, and they sang in time as they skipped:

> "The big ship sailed on the Alley-alley-O
>   The Alley-alley-O
>   The Alley-alley-O
> The big ship sailed on the Alley-alley-O
> On the fifth day of September."

The rope slapped the road at every beat of the song. My sister left her friends when she saw me, and stood apart. She didn't smile or anything like that. She held her own skipping rope in her hand—one she'd had as a present for her birthday. It had bright wooden handles and a glittering weight halfway along the cord to help it turn. My sister put her finger in her mouth and looked at me very carefully for a long time, and then she ran up the road, her dark hair flying and bouncing as she ran. I never saw her again.

I think of Swindon as a Victorian town. The office in which I worked was enormous, its ceiling so high that it sent back an echo of everything we said, so that we worked almost without speaking. Even then the air seemed curiously hollow and trembling, as if we sat in a tiled cave. But that might well have been because of the darkness. I remember that we had fishtails of gaslight flaring on the walls, although this may not be true and I am inventing where memory is empty. Certainly there was dust every-where—on the spiked files of our invoices, settling on the white pages of our ledgers, dust filming the polished black of our shoes as each morning we entered the building. I stayed five weeks in Swindon.

I lodged with Mr. and Mrs. Guthrie—it was all arranged before I arrived. Arthur Guthrie was a clerk in the same office, a stolid man, pale, unemotional, deep-voiced. He had the most beautiful handwriting I've ever seen, and I used to copy it on odd bits of paper whenever I had the chance. We walked to work together in the mornings and home together in the evenings, through the used streets of the town. I liked him, and I liked Mrs. Guthrie, too.

Arthur Guthrie kept canaries in his garden, in a lean-to aviary built against the back wall of his house. On sunny evenings, the tiny yellow birds sang so stridently that the house seemed to throb. When they sang like this, Arthur Guthrie would lift his head and listen intently, but he never said anything. I got into the habit of going into the aviary after supper. I'd clean out the cages and give the birds fresh seed and water. It was something to do.

One evening, returning indoors from the aviary, I heard them quarrelling, Arthur and Mrs. Guthrie. They weren't shouting, and for a time I thought they were speaking ordinarily, but when I heard my name I listened more carefully. It was a nice little house, the Guthries', and late in the day the kitchen was filled with light. It faced west, I expect. I looked through the open door and saw Arthur sitting stiffly on a wooden chair, his elbows on the table, his wife opposite him. They didn't know I was there. There was a yellow-and-white checked cloth on the table, and dishes from the evening meal were stacked neatly in the middle.

"He's only a boy," said Mrs. Guthrie.

"He may be," Arthur said, "but he's a nuisance. I can't stand him. I can't stand his chattering, nor the way he copies my handwriting. I can't go into the aviary without him following behind. I didn't want him here to start with. It was your idea from the first."

"There's nothing we can do now," said Mrs. Guthrie. "Give him a few weeks. Perhaps he'll find friends of his own."

"If he was my own boy," Arthur said, "I wouldn't mind, I can see that. But he isn't. I don't want a son. A lodger is what I thought he was. He'll have to go."

"You'll have to tell him," Mrs. Guthrie said. "I won't tell him. That's a man's job."

I went outside quietly and walked about the garden until I felt better. Then I went in the house.

"Hullo, boy," said Arthur. "Do you want a cup of tea?"

I could see him struggling to be fair to me.

"No, thanks," I said, "I think I'll take a walk down the road."

I could feel my face pretending to smile.

"That's right," said Mrs. Guthrie. "Enjoy yourself."

For the life of me, I can't remember her first name, but it was something quite ordinary, like Ethel or Margaret.

I collected my wages that Friday night, and the next morning I told Mrs. Guthrie I was going home for the weekend. I didn't see Arthur. It didn't take long to pack my bag and I was at the station in less than ten minutes, but I didn't go home. Instead, I caught a train to London. When I got there, somebody told me where the Y.M.C.A. was. I took a room there, and in a week I was working in a stock-broker's office in the City.

Three years I was in London, loving every minute of it. In those days, there was a spaciousness about the place, and a good-humored assumption by its inhabitants that they were better in every way than people anywhere else. I believed this. People lived in the heart of London then, not, as now, on the outskirts, the center a lit emptiness after business is over. I began a new life in London, forgetting almost completely what had happened to me before. I moved from job to job, urgently and expertly. I did my growing in London, became tall and elegant, a fashionable young man as far as money would allow. At last, when it was time for me to leave the place, I even had a new name.

The summer of 1939 was brilliant, cloudless. In the city squares, the plane trees had put out their leaves early, always a good sign, and after lunch I would saunter back to the office through gaudy sunlight filtering green and gold among the trees. I worked then for a firm of lawyers whose main function was the management of several large estates of houses—old properties most of them, divided into flats. Three days a week, I went out collecting rents, and on Thursdays and Fridays I did the paperwork connected with my houses. There were three of us at this, and we operated a sweet little fraud that brought us in several illegal pounds every month.

One Thursday, a little late from lunch, I reached the office and realized that we had been caught. The place was silent and miserable, my friend Edwards white-faced and despairing at his desk. He looked as though he'd been crying.

"So there you are, there you are," said the chief clerk. "Mr. Fawcett will want your ledgers in a few minutes."

The old fool was so excited that he almost skipped as he spoke. We'd not been too kind to him, Edwards and I. I smiled at him cheerfully.

"They're all ready," I said, "except the final balance, and that can wait. I'll take them in now."

I picked up my ledgers, put them under my arm, walked

out of the room. I went calmly along the corridor, down two flights of stairs, and away. I'd had to leave an almost new raincoat behind, but that was no worry. The ledgers went into a wastebasket in Oxford Street, just before I walked into a recruiting office and joined the Army. Although the recruiting officer wanted me to be more ambitious, I joined the infantry. I knew exactly what I wanted. In a conveniently short time I was Private Sutton, G.A., at a training camp in Wiltshire. I was seventeen years old.

The war began before we were trained: I hadn't thought of war. Early in the winter, we were sent north to Blackpool, living in huts at the edge of that holiday town. I had enjoyed my first weeks in the Army. What I liked best was the intricate ritual of the barrack square, the perfection of rhythmical movement as line after line marched and counter-marched, the precise order firm and unbroken, despite the increasing complexity of our tramping patterns. It was almost better when we got to Blackpool, for we arose there in the winter mornings, formed our long columns in the breathing dark, and moved out into the streets. The town was asleep and half dead; only the hibernating proprietors lived in the small hotels and boarding houses, waiting for the war to end and for plentiful summer to come. We swung into the town, not a light showing, and marched along the miles of seafront, the waves on one hand and the summer shops, their windows boarded against the wind that blew in from the Atlantic, on the other. As we marched, our heels would hammer the scatterings of little pebbles thrown over the road by the sea, and they'd rattle away in step with us, like the ghosts of kettledrums. In that hypnotic rhythm, we stepped away our days, perfectly, mindlessly.

Most of the boys in my company were badly educated, some quite illiterate. In my hut, I alone wrote and read fluently, and my Sundays were taken up with writing letters to mothers and girls. It wasn't long before my proficiency was noted and I was transferred to the company office. My marching days were over.

There was not enough work to keep me busy, and most afternoons I went to the zoo in the Winter Gardens. I used to visit a tawny brown puma, kept in a pen with other big cats. He sat alert at the back of the cage, missing nothing, tense for the chance that he knew must one day come. Or he walked with fluid beauty, up and down, up and down, always at the back of the cage, as far away from us as he could get. He was a great cat, and I think of him still from time to time.

In the spring, when we left for Scotland, I was a full corporal. The routine of the company office was at my fingertips. In small ways, I already had some power.

We lived under canvas. I had a tent of my own, near a stream at the edge of camp. So smooth was the run of water that it seemed not to move, but at night, in the poor light of the moon or in the near-darkness of the reflected sky, the ripples of its steady flowing could be recognized. I sat there every night, near the water.

I read a lot in Scotland. The town had a superb library, and I went through it like a plague. Had we stayed there a few more months, I should have read every book they had.

By this time, most of the work in the office was left to me. I made decisions, I acted, the strokes of the pen were mine. I was a sergeant long before we went to Africa.

What I most admired about the Army was the way in which the system was simplified and made effective. Life at first was difficult and ritualistic, the day filled with tiny ceremonies which existed only in order that men should have something to do, or because they were thoughtlessly continued long after the reasons for their performance had been eroded. But as the war became more fierce and desperate, so, too, did life become simpler and more pragmatic. I learned that from the Army. I learned to profit from all opportunities, and there were many, and I walked very much alone.

I was a warrant officer when I left in 1946. I could have

stayed on. Three times I was offered a commission. But I had outgrown the Army. This way and that, I had made some money. I put my money to work. It grew, it multiplied, it worked for me.

My secretary is a sensible woman, not young. She's competent, tactful, doesn't try to run things herself. She has come back to a career because time was hanging a little heavily, I think. Her husband is a doctor, and she has two sons at Cambridge. She's in her early forties.

Last week, I said to her, "Mrs. Braithwaite, forty-two years are long enough for a man to live."

I can't think why I said such a thing. It certainly wasn't in my mind to say it. She was amused, knowing that I'm past fifty.

"You'll be saying that when you're eighty," she said, "and I've no doubt you'll still be sharper than anyone else in sight."

She gets a good salary, that woman. I'm a rich man.

My father was forty-two when he died.

Perhaps I should go back there, to the place where I was a child. I never have, although once or twice I've been fairly near. My sister, if she's alive, would be forty-three now. She might have children—my nephews and nieces.

About ten years ago, when I was buying a lot of land for investment, I had a sudden urge to get hold of Edgar Martin's farm. Farmland was comparatively cheap then, although I knew its value was increasing and I'd already got hold of three or four very large places—two estates in Scotland and one in Sussex among them. They made a lot of money later on, when I sold them. Edgar Martin's place would have been useless to me. It was only about thirty acres, not worth troubling with. But I thought seriously about it until I realized that I was influenced by forgotten things, the river pool, the memory of Edgar holding aloft those shining eels on the salt marsh, old, intangible summers.

I'll never go back; I know that.

Lately though, at night, on the edge of sleep, when the mind is undefended, I have seen again those grasses at the cemetery's verge more vividly fresh and green than they were long ago. Luminous, possessing the obsessive clarity of things seen in dreams, they let me trace at will their characteristic outlines, to recognize with the faultless certainty of my youthful knowledge each typical specimen. They hold themselves quietly for my recognition, and I make a ceremony of their names.

And this morning, as I shaved, I could hear those names clearly under the hum of the razor: couch, perennial rye grass, false oat, timothy, meadow foxtail, quaking grass, sheep's fescue and red fescue, erect brome, cocksfoot, crested dog's-tail, sweet vernal grass.

The Highland Boy

The first greyhound I ever owned was a black-brindled dog called Highland Boy. He was a small dog, weighing perhaps fifty-three pounds, and his coat was a dull black with sparse streaks of rust-colored hair running through it. He was not attractive at first glance, and his expression was at once conciliatory and untrustworthy. I had known him for a year before I became his owner, because he belonged to my Uncle Cedric.

My Uncle Cedric owned a tobacconist's and confectionery shop in Victoria Road, very near to our house, and it was my habit to visit this shop on Saturday evenings to buy a quarter of a pound of chocolate caramels. Cedric would take a paper bag as big as a pillowcase, and thrusting his hand into all the glass jars around him, would fill it with a sweet assortment of flavors enough to last a week. This situation was not as perfect as it seems, for Bertie Christopher soon discovered my Saturday evening fortune, and he and his gang would perch like a row of twelve-year-old vultures on the railings opposite my uncle's shop, waiting for me to emerge. Fighting was out of the question since the very weight of the sweets was an embarrassment. I used to hover patiently behind the door of the shop until something broke momentarily their brooding concentration, and then I'd run for it. Sprinting and jinking like a startled buck, I'd break past three or four fairly easily. After that it was head down and knock my way through. Most Saturdays at that time I could be found fingering a swollen eye or some other temporary and violent blemish, gloomily eating a chocolate-covered almond or a marzipan whirl, wondering if it was worth it.

Highland Boy was often in the shop with my Uncle Cedric on Saturday evenings. They would both have been to the unlicensed track at the top of the town, and my uncle would usually be staring in a bewildered fashion at Highland Boy. All the dog ever did was to whisk his thin tail once or twice and then look shyly and resignedly at the floor. I often thought my uncle took a kind of defiant pride in the dog.

Uncle Cedric was a tall, thin man, almost completely bald although he was only twenty-eight. He had the most ferocious eyebrows I have ever seen, and my grandmother said that if he were to comb them back over his bare skull they would offer more than adequate compensation. She never said this in Cedric's hearing because he was sensitive. Cedric wore checked suits, and he would stand with his hands, his fingertips anyway, in the little pockets of his waistcoat, which made his elbows stick out like the stubby wings of a sparrow and his shoulders lift almost up to his ears. He was mild and slow-moving enough normally, but phenomenally strong and brisk when angry. Nobody cared to argue with Cedric. I once saw him argue with three Irishmen who had decided to contest, as a matter of entertainment, a debt of honor. Cedric stood against a shop-window in case they should attempt to attack him from behind and set about dealing with them.

"B'Jasus, he's a daisy," cried the admiring Irishmen as they reeled and staggered away. "Didja ever see the dint he gave Paddy, now?"

They all four went into a public house, and I was left to mind Cedric's van.

On a golden Saturday in late August, at eight-thirty in the evening, I went as usual for my trove of sugar. Bertie Christopher and his gang watched my every step with cold, un-blinking eyes. The shop door was open, and Cedric and

Highland Boy stood inside. I knew at once that there was some serious trouble. The dog was absolutely still, head and tail hanging low, and he did not give me even a hint of a greeting. I looked up at Cedric. Great, silent tears were rolling down his face.

"What's wrong?" I asked. "Uncle Cedric, what's the matter?"

He was shaking with anger, but his voice was remote and controlled.

"This bloody dog," he said, "has kept the bookmakers in affluence, with my money, since the day I bought him. I have been involved in many a disgraceful and undignified scene because of the deceitful manner in which he races, people believing that I, in some devilish way, have control over his actions. All this I have put up with because of my love of animals. But he has killed my cat, and that is the end."

Cedric loved his cat, a large, somnolent, ginger creature. This was gasping tragedy. I looked at Highland Boy. His eye was mild and distant, and there were flecks of ginger fur about his mouth.

A small, nervous man came in for cigarettes, and Cedric wept unashamed as he served him with a packet of the wrong brand.

"What are you going to do?" I asked.

"Take him out of my sight, boy," said Cedric. "I make him over to you as a present. Tomorrow I'll give you his pedigree and registration papers, but take him out of my sight."

I hooked my fingers behind Highland Boy's collar and went. Bertie Christopher was surprised enough to let me pass without a struggle, and then Highland Boy and I trotted down the garden and into the house.

My father was sitting in his armchair reading Dickens, which is what he always did when he wasn't busy.

"What's this?" he said.

"A dog," I said, "Highland Boy."

"He needs feeding. You can keep him in the wash-house," said my father. The dog looked at him, and he looked at the dog. They liked each other.

So began my career as a greyhound owner.

I used to get up very early each morning and exercise that dog over the moors. I became hard and stringy, able to run for prodigious distances without distress, but Highland Boy seemed completely unaffected. When I had enough money—the fee was five shillings—I would enter him for a race on one of the unlicensed tracks either in our town or in one of the neighboring towns. Neither he nor I was popular on these tracks.

I have thought since that the dog was an imaginative genius. There may be ways of reducing a race to chaos that he didn't invent, but I doubt it. Sometimes he would shoot away with every appearance of running an orthodox and blameless five hundred and twenty-five yards, which was the usual length of a race, only to feel lonely up there in front. He would wait for the second dog and gambol along beside him, smiling and twisting in an ecstasy of friendship. This commonly so upset the other dog that he ran wide, turned round, or lost ground so rapidly that he was effectively out of the running; I'd have to avoid the owner of such a dog for months. He won a solitary race, in Aberdare, in so strange a fashion that I was almost ashamed to collect the prize money. Running with a controlled abandon which left the honest journeymen who were his competitors far behind, he got to within a foot of the winning post and stopped dead. The second dog, laboring along twenty lengths behind, ran heavily into him and knocked Highland Boy over the line. Four Chinamen, heavy and regular gamblers, leaped and capered as they ran for the bookmakers. They were the most scrutable men I ever saw, and the only men who ever made a killing on my dog. After this race,

Benny Evans, who was the handicapper at the track, suggested that it might be sensible if I kept my dog away until people's memories grew dim. I could see his point.

Every September, as if to give an added splendor to the death of summer, a great open competition was held at the Tredegar track, twelve miles away over the hills. The prize was twenty-five pounds and a silver cup. My Uncle Cedric now possessed a marvellous dog, the beautiful Special Request, and he would certainly enter him. He spoke to my father and me of his well-founded hopes.

"When I went over to Ireland," he said, "to buy this dog from Father Seamus Riordan, I was assured there wasn't a dog to touch him. And they were right. That silver cup is as good as in my hands, barring accidents, and the twenty-five pounds too."

He beamed at the glorious tan-and-white greyhound, silken-coated and sided like a bream.

"He's a beauty," I said.

"You ought to take your dog. I'll pay for his entry," my father said.

"Why not?" said Cedric, with the large generosity of a man who knows he is not to be affected by the decisions of lesser men.

I went over to Tredegar on the bus, on the Thursday night of the qualifying races. Highland Boy behaved admirably, running second to a very good dog which had been specially imported from Bristol. This meant that he went into the semifinals the next evening. Cedric's dog won his heat very easily and broke the track record. Almost everybody from our town was on him to win the final, and our hopes were high.

When we got to the track on the Friday evening, we found that the two semifinals were to be held last on the program. Cedric was amused to find that our dogs were in the same race, Special Request in Box 6, which was lucky since he was a superbly fast starter, and Highland Boy in Box 3. The first three dogs in each race would go on to the final, to be held a week later. I knew I had no chance. High-land Boy was too small to stand the buffeting that would certainly go on in the middle of the track.

"Never mind," said Cedric, "he's done very well to get as far as this."

The lights were shining on the track by the time our race was announced. I went down to the paddock and put the racing coat with the large number three on it around High-land Boy, taking care not to fasten it too tightly under his stomach. He seemed only half the size of the other dogs. I felt like crying. I put his racing muzzle on. He was unper-turbed, perfectly at ease among the eager whining of the other dogs. The stewards made me wear a long white coat to walk him down to the boxes. It was too long and I had to hold it up with one hand and everybody laughed.

"It's ridiculous to allow a boy to put his dog in an impor-tant race like this," said Paul Davies, a thin lame man, as we walked down the track. "Particularly a dog like that thing; he can ruin any race."

My uncle gave him a red look.

"The cure for your lameness, Paul, is to break the good leg," he said.

Paul, whose disability had given him guile and cunning, thought of the three Irishmen and gulped.

"I hope you don't think I was talking of your nephew here," he said. "Why, this boy is a credit. He has a real sense of vocation and will be just like you, Ced, in a couple of years."

We walked silently down to the line of six boxes, put our dogs in one by one, and ran across the field over to the finish, so that we would be ready to collect them after the race.

They flew out of the traps, and Special Request was well in front by the second bend. I couldn't even see my dog. On the back straight he was last and not moving very freely, but as they hit the last bend he began to run, weaving through the field with breathtaking speed. I was proud of him. He finished third, well behind the first two, but he was in the final.

Now I had a week before the great day. I gave Highland Boy two raw eggs a day, fed him on minced beef before putting him in his straw, walked him until my feet were raw. He didn't seem an ounce different.

On the night of the final we went in a hired bus. We carried with us all the loose money in the town, and we were thick with strategies for getting good odds from the bookmakers. I sat in a front seat, behind the driver where I could get a good view of the road, and Highland Boy sat between my feet. I wore my best suit, the one with a gray stripe, and I wasn't going to wear a long white coat whatever happened.

We got to the track, and I waited about through the dragging tedium of the earlier races. I could see my uncle's friends, jovial with expectation, their eyes full of money. Highland Boy was drawn in Box 1, a good position if he got away quickly enough, right on the rail. Cedric's dog was in Box 5, which was perfectly all right for him. He was a big dog and could barge his way through.

I went down to the paddock in a dream, my fingers shaking so that I couldn't fasten the racing coat, and Cedric did it for me.

"Good luck, Uncle," I said.

"He'll dawdle it," said Cedric. "My Special Request will dawdle it. The only interesting question is, Who's going to be second?"

I put Highland Boy into the first box and he went in like a gentleman. When I popped around the front to have a look at him, he gave me a serious and apologetic glance, and I knew how he felt.

"It doesn't matter, you've done well," I said.

The bell went, and the hare began its run from behind the starting line. I could have sworn that Highland Boy's box opened seconds before the others, but I know that's impossible. He was fifteen yards clear at the end of the first straight and fled around the bend, tracking so closely to the inner fence that I thought he would leave the color of his skin on every inch of it. He coiled and stretched with brilliant suppleness and vigor, throwing his length into a stride like a flying dive, balling himself tight, his back arched high, then unleashing again. I knew, everybody in the stadium knew, that the race was over before it was halfway run. My dog won by fifteen easy lengths, and I had collected him, put on his lead, and begun to walk away when the second dog reached us, panting and exhausted. I was spring-heeled with elation, but I held my face stiff because I knew it was wrong of me to feel even remotely happy. I thought of Uncle Cedric, his pockets full of red and white ribbon he'd bought especially to decorate the cup. I wondered how we could go home to our friends to tell them that all their money was lost, that the wrong dog had won the cup. I looked down at Highland Boy. The muscles on his quarters were shivering, but he seemed all right otherwise. He was a heartless dog.

They made me walk him around the track, and he danced on his toes every inch of it. He knew he'd won. They gave me a check for twenty-five pounds and a dented cup, said to be silver. Everybody cheered derisively, except the relieved bookmakers and the silent, ominous party of my uncle's friends. People jeered Uncle Cedric, and he had no reply. We filed into our cheerless coach. Nobody congratulated me. I held the unwanted cup on my knee until it began to get heavy, and then I put it under the seat.

We sat together, Uncle Cedric and I, on the seat nearest the door, and Highland Boy coiled himself into a tactful ball at our feet. My uncle put Special Request on the seat between us and then hunched into his overcoat, dark with gloom, unmoving except for the fingers of his left hand, which absentmindedly fondled the folded ear of his defeated champion. Behind us, from the back seat where he sat with four of his friends, I could hear the bitter voice of big Carl Jenkins. He spoke quietly at first, but now his voice grew heavy and bold.

He was very nasty. He said that although he had known my uncle to be the biggest crook in four valleys, he had not thought Cedric would swindle his own friends of their hard-earned money. This, said Carl Jenkins, was the lowest of my uncle's many abominable tricks. He reasoned that my uncle was bald only because nothing as honest and natural as hair would live on him. "And," added Carl Jenkins, "like master, like dog. We all know that Highland Boy could never be trusted."

There was a lot of muttered support for this opinion, and one or two bolder spirits began to threaten my uncle with violence. He sat unmoved, as if deaf.

"Oh, he's a fly one," said Carl Jenkins. "You won't find many as fly as Cedric. Have you ever known him to do an honest day's work? Never. All he does is sit in his shop, growing rich and planning the schemes and tricks by which he robs his friends of their money. He pretends," continued Carl Jenkins with a sour irony, "that the dog belongs to the boy there, but we all know the boy will do whatever Cedric tells him."

The bus swung slowly round the corner at the end of Bennett Street and hung above the hill into High Street. My uncle tapped the driver on the shoulder as a signal that he should stop. The bus sidled in to the curb.

"How much money did he take over to Tredegar," trumpeted Carl Jenkins, swollen with eloquence and sorrow, "money which his trusting friends had asked him to put on that fine dog Special Request, which would have won if he hadn't been up to his criminal tricks? How much money did you steal from us, Cedric?"

The bus stopped, and my uncle stood up. His smile was genial and terrible. He looked slowly about him, nodding his head here and there, as if thoughtfully recognizing certain people in front of him. His hands were deep in the pockets of his overcoat.

"Jump off, boy," he said, "and trot home all the way. The dog could do with a loosener."

He didn't look at me at all. I scuffled under the seat for the rolling trophy, grabbed Highland Boy's lead, and prepared to jump.

"Two hundred and forty-one pounds," my uncle said, very mildly. "I took two hundred and forty-one pounds to Tredegar with me tonight, and a hundred of them were my own."

He sighed deeply.

"Has anybody on this bus lost as much as I have?" he asked. "A hundred pounds? Because I left the whole of that money, the whole two hundred and forty-one pounds, in the hands of the bookmakers. I've cheated nobody, and I've lost more money than anybody else. If there is a villain, then it's Highland Boy. But he ran a good race, he ran a fine race, and he beat us all. Hurry up, boy. And now, Carl Jenkins, I'll push your nose through the back of your neck and tie your lying mouth in a knot."

As I jumped from the bus, already moving slowly, I saw my uncle advancing majestically upon his enemy, but although I pounded downhill after the bus, I saw no more.

I went home and told my father. He was sitting by the fire reading P. G. Wodehouse, which is what he did when he was very happy, usually on Saturday evenings and at Christmas, but when I told him that Uncle Cedric was fighting Carl Jenkins in the bus, he got up, put on his hat and coat, and left. I could not remember my father ever having left the house at night before.

Later, after perhaps an hour, he returned.

"Did you see Uncle Cedric?" I asked.

My father nodded.

"Was the fight over?"

My father thought about that one; he was a very precise man.

"It was all over as far as Carl Jenkins was concerned," he answered, "but there were one or two others your uncle felt aggrieved with. However, the police were about to arrive, and I persuaded Cedric that he ought to catch the late train to Cardiff, to stay with his cousins, just for a while. Now you'd better go to bed.''

For some weeks my grandmother kept behind the counter in my uncle's shop. When I went on Saturdays for my quarter of a pound of chocolate caramels, she would weigh them out with hairbreadth accuracy, five to the ounce, as if I were any casual customer. Life seemed to have lost much of its savor, and I was too dispirited to avoid Bertie Christopher wholeheartedly. I took to fighting him so often that I soon knew every move he was likely to make, although his right swing was always risky. In the end we knocked each other into a grudging friendship, and when Uncle Cedric came back from Cardiff after a month, I rather liked sharing my Saturday candy with Bertie and the other boys.

By that time my father had taken Highland Boy to live in the house. Without anybody saying anything, it was somehow agreed that his racing career was over. He had a basket down by the fire, but most of the time he'd be leaning against my father's knees, fawning on my old man in the most shameless manner. It used to be sickening to see them together, watching them walk down the garden with leisurely dignity, or stand silently together while they contemplated some gentle problem. It was annoying to see Highland Boy a reformed scoundrel, wearing his drab color with the proud humility and decency of a deacon.

He lived with us for another twelve years, dying the month after Bertie Christopher went to work in London, but it was longer than that before I owned another greyhound.

The Mallard

This village is rich in ponds. I don't mean the enormous gravel pits, some of them many acres in area, which lie some miles to the west, although these are very remarkable. Once or twice during the war I flew above them at night and they were clearly visible, great sheets of calm, much lighter than the dark farmland and the little town they encircled. I like the gravel pits. A lot of wild ducks live on them—garganey, teal, the little black-and-white tufted duck, and of course the ubiquitous mallard.

But the ponds we have in the village are small and hidden. Driving through, I doubt if you'd notice one of them. Fed by the narrow streams that drain any water off the downs, they stand at the corners of fields, hidden by clusters of unimportant trees. They are rarely more than twenty feet or so across, or more than three feet deep. I have one at the end of my paddock, where my two acres join Rasbridge's land. I suppose it's his pond rather than mine, since his house is very near it.

Come to that, this house of mine is built on what used to be a pond. When I bought the site I had the pond filled in, felled the enormous elms that fringed it, and dug a new channel for the stream. Where my front lawn is now, that was the pond.

There were mallard on it then, quite a number. Old Normanton, who lives up the lane in a converted barn, was out cutting the grass in one of the fields, Rasbridge's fields now but they weren't then, when he saw over his shoulder the whirling blades behind his tractor cut straight through a mallard duck. He stopped and jumped off. She was dead of course. She had sat tight on a nest of twelve eggs and the blades had sliced her. Oddly, the eggs were unharmed, and old Normanton put them in the hedge in his cap. When he went home for lunch he put them under a broody hen and they all hatched out in two or three days. Later, he clipped their wings and they all seemed to live fairly happily on the pond where my house is. By the time I filled the pond in, only one old drake was left from that original settlement. He could fly, but in a curious lopsided way, sideways to the face of the pond. Then, as he landed, he flicked his body somehow, so that he hit the water facedown, or stomach-down anyway.

They didn't move, these mallard, all through the time we were building the house. I think they were the descendants of some of Normanton's ducks and of an old Khaki Campbell duck which was still around. She was absolutely tame, of course, and so much the leader of the flock that they all followed her example. Some of the young duck were very much bigger than ordinary mallard, and a lot of them were paler too, and these were her children and grandchildren. When we moved in eventually I had a lot of fun with these birds. They are pretty intelligent, are ducks. At night they used to lie around on the new banks of the stream and as I walked past them they'd gossip to me. I knew them individually. They were extraordinarily different. Every day the baker used to deliver a couple of stale loaves, just to feed them. There were two young drakes able to catch pieces of bread in their beaks while they were swimming, as if they were performing seals. We had some trouble occasionally. Youngsters would stone the ducks, particularly the baby ducks in May and June, and this used to make me mad, but in a way I could understand it too. After about three years the old boy who farmed most of the land around here retired, and Rasbridge moved in.

The first time I met Rasbridge was over the affair of the

poplar trees. I saw old Normanton, who stayed on to work
for Rasbridge, planting half a dozen young silver poplars at
the edge of my paddock and I went over to have a word
with him. It isn't that I don't like the trees, but it was
thoughtless to plant them there without asking how I felt
about them. I have a marvellous view from the end of my
little field, right over the flat, rich arable of Rasbridge's
acres, on to Slindon Woods at the edge of the downs, and
then the bare curve of the hills themselves. In May, as it is
now, the downs gleam like chromium in the sun where the
plow has laid the white chalk open. In two years, or less
even, the quick-growing poplars would have taken most of
this from me. I said as much to Normanton. He's a nice old
man, real Sussex. I've known him for years.

"You're right," he said. "I never thought of that."

"Do you think I could have a word with your boss about
them?" I asked.

" 'Tisn't worth it," he said. "No, you leave that to me,
look, and 'twill be all right."

I left it to him. I saw him in the pub a few days later and
he came over to me, shamefaced. I let him take his time
over things because he's not a man you can hurry, and in
the end he told me all about it.

"No luck about them poplars," he said.

I didn't say anything. The technique is to let him assume
you know all about everything and then he doesn't have the
embarrassment of explaining.

"No," he said, "no luck."

He took a long pull at his beer.

" 'Tis his wife," he said, "but she shouldn't have said
what she did. I told Mr. Rasbridge straight. That house of
Mr. Simmonds', I said, is a pretty little house and Mrs.
Rasbridge hasn't got any call to say what she did. A terrible
little modern house she called it. She can only see it from
two of her upstairs windows anyway."

I laughed. I didn't think I cared what she thought, but I
must have.

"Have another pint," I said to old Normanton.

"Thank you, Mr. Simmonds," he said. "That'll be lovely."

We both looked out of the window at the dusty Sunday cars racing to the sea.

"Beans he's got in that field," said old Normanton, "dwarf beans. We're growing them for the frozen-food people. Very particular they are, make us use some very strong sprays to keep the weeds down. I shouldn't be surprised, then, if those trees, young like that, was to take permanent harm from a strong dose of spray."

He looked at me guilelessly before he smiled. I could see suddenly what he had been like as a boy.

Rasbridge introduced himself to me a week or so later. He was a tall, thin man with a bony and rather refined face. He spoke quickly, with real energy. His teeth were large and yellow and he wore a gray moustache.

"Sorry about those trees," he said. "Didn't think you'd object. Make a very necessary windbreak, you know. That's a damnably draughty house we have."

The house had been there for five hundred years and had its old trees all around it.

"Oh, that's all right," I said, and I smiled as falsely as he did.

One night in the summer I took out my thin pruning saw and cut a neat circle around the base of every one of those poplars. I felt like a murderer when I did it, because the sap was strong and under the bark the flesh was wet and living. I painted the soft, white wood with some stuff I bought for the purpose and walked home whistling. All the trees died except one, and that's so maimed and runt I can scarcely bear to look at it. They rotted at the bottom and the young leaves shriveled and died. In November a strong wind blew all five poisoned trees to the ground and they were never replaced.

But by that time my ducks were gone.

We had a lot of young mallard that year and it was the

habit of people in the village to bring up their small children to see them. There's nothing quite as engaging as ducklings and when I saw two strange youngsters in my garden, a boy of about ten and a girl some years younger, looking at the ducks, I wasn't surprised. They were pleasant children, confident and polite, and I liked them. I showed them all my parlor tricks, how I called the birds down to feed them, how I soaked the bread for them in a large bowl. They were charming children.

That evening I heard young voices calling from Rasbridge's garden.

"Bill bill bill bill bill!" they called, exactly as I did, and a group of young, unattached drakes cocked their glossy heads and took off for Rasbridge's pond. I saw them feather over the tall horse chestnut that shades his water and imagined them dropping down with a flutter of their braking wings. My ducklings grew up and, in the natural way of things, dispersed. A number of older birds went too. By summer's end I had less than half a dozen mallard on my stream and soon they went too. In the colder mornings I could hear them call from Rasbridge's yard. They were probably being fed grain there. My stream is too small to support many birds anyway. I was left with the old Khaki Campbell. Her domesticity kept her with me. She died about the time the poplars were blown down. I found her in the stream. She was very old and had been lame for weeks. Perhaps she hadn't enjoyed life without her flock around her.

I've never had birds permanently on my water since, although I always get a pair or two come over in March, bring up their two broods, and go back again to Rasbridge's. One of the ducks I've grown to know well. She's a small, dark bird with the loudest and most demanding voice I've ever heard. When she's sitting, and I've never been able to find her nest, she flies in about six-thirty in the morning and demands to be fed. I have it all ready for her and get up in my dressing gown, go down to the garden, and feed her.

She talks to me all the time she eats, chuckling and muttering confidentially. A duck can't look at you directly, since their eyes are set at the sides of their heads, so they turn to look at you with one beady eye. This gives them a comically knowing expression. When she'd see there was no more food she'd race over the lawn and plunge into the water, throwing it ecstatically over her back and head as she rocked vigorously backward and forward. Then she'd squawk once or twice, swim up the stream, and take off. I'd see her circle the house, her neck outstretched, her hammerhead set at an angle.

"Bill bill bill!" I'd call, and she'd give one raucous answer before flying swiftly off, her stubby wings flashing.

In the warm afternoons the young drakes come over and sit on the lawn or indulge in loud splashing horseplay in the water. They are incredibly handsome in their breeding plumage, reminding me of groups of very young men dressed in their finery, parading for no other purpose than the gallant manipulation of their fashionable clothes. My friends and I were rather like this, when we were sixteen or seventeen.

When I was sixteen I thought I would be a great athlete. I didn't know whether to be a footballer or a boxer, but I trained assiduously every day. I belonged to a good amateur boxing club in those days and often represented it at tournaments. I was a slender boy, nearly always taller than my opponents, and I had been taught to box in the orthodox way, upright, elegant, left hand out. I was quite good at it. Sometimes, however, something startling happened to me. If I were very confident, or if I were hurt, my style changed suddenly, and without my being able to do anything about it. I seemed to drop into a crouching, urgent stance, my feet close together, and my left hand swinging low across my body. It would hook to the body and head of the boy I was fighting with an accuracy and ferocity that had nothing to do with me. It was like being taken over;

perhaps it was a sort of inspiration. Anyway, it frightened me. At last I spoke to my father about it. It was no good going to him for pleasant conversation—you had to have something serious to say before you dared bother him—but he was marvellous when you were in trouble. He listened very carefully, nodding now and then in encouragement and understanding. When I had finished he looked at me quietly and said, "If I were you, I'd give it up now."

So I did. It was very easy and direct. I often think of things like this when I look at the young drakes.

Last Tuesday my dark mallard duck didn't come to be fed as usual. I got up early just the same. There had been some shooting the night before in the fields behind the house, but I hadn't taken much notice of it. Rasbridge's boy after pigeons I thought. I got the car out when it became obvious my duck wasn't hungry, and drove through the early lanes on the downs.

Just before lunch, about eleven o'clock I suppose, I went down to the end of my paddock and found the duck. She was dead. She had been shot through the breast and she was dead and stiff. I picked her up. She was unbelievably light and her poor feathers were dry and harsh. Her eye was a blob of excrement. That morning I had seen in one of the lanes the body of a hare which had been knocked by a car. A crow was standing on it, tearing at the soft belly. I had accepted this as one of the things that happened, but I was shaking angry as I brought the duck home. I buried her in the garden, knowing how useless it was.

I had a bad night that night, unusual for me, and I didn't sleep much until morning. When I got up I didn't want breakfast, so I went into the garden. The baker's van was down the road a little way. He was probably delivering to Mrs. Rogers. I walked down the drive and leaned on the gate. Rasbridge drove up in his green estate car. When he saw me, he pulled up and leapt out.

"A pleasant day, Simmonds," he said.

I opened the gate and walked toward him.

"Things are beginning to move," he said. "I've just been over to see my wheat and it looks good, really good."

He looked over the gate at my roses.

"By jove," he said, "your garden is looking very well too."

He smiled at me as if the sun shone for him alone.

"By the way," he said, "I've had to cull some of the mallard. Far too many of them, you know—they're keeping me poor."

I don't know what I said, but he stopped laughing and swung at me. It was pitiable really. I'd hit him twice before his fist had finished its backswing, and a slow trickle of blood came from his nose. Then suddenly I was crouching and weaving, my left hooking him to head and body so hard I thought he'd snap. Whatever it was I had thought buried in me was not dead. There was no need for the right hand I gave him as he went down. I would have stamped on him, I think, if the baker hadn't grabbed me. Strangely enough I wasn't upset. I looked down at Rasbridge, at his yellow face with the quick swelling on the temple above his right eyebrow, the bruise on the cheekbone and the right side of his jaw. I suppose I must have hit him seventeen or eighteen times.

The baker, kneeling near him, looked up at me, his eyes round and staring.

"You'd better bring him into my terrible little modern house," I said.

"No sir," said the man, "I'll take him home."

When he could stand, we helped Rasbridge into his car and the baker drove him home. I've heard nothing about him since then and that was two days ago.

My wife came home from town and I told her all about it. She's a good girl and didn't say very much, but this afternoon she asked me if I thought the life of a duck was worth such a disaster.

"Too damn right it is," I said, but I knew what she

meant. We've been over to Rasbridge's several times for a meal or drinks, and they've been here too. I like those two kids of his very much. I suppose he was entitled to think I was his friend. Sometimes I think it must have looked very comic, Rasbridge and I brawling outside the front gate. After all I'm fifty-two and he must be at least three years older. But the way I hit him wasn't funny at all. I saw myself unawares in the hall mirror this morning and for the first time in my life I look older than my years.

I haven't been outside the house for two days. I don't know what to do.

A Big Night

I used to train at the Ex-Servicemen's Club three nights a week, Tuesdays, Wednesdays, and Fridays. Training began at six, but I was always late on Tuesdays and Wednesdays because of homework. I used to like getting there a bit late. As I hurried through the long passage that ran beside the room where the old, dry miners—hardly any of them ex-servicemen—were drinking away their age and disappointment, I would hear above me the slithering feet of the other boys as they moved around the ring or the punch-bags and the pungent smell of the liniment would come greenly down the stairs to meet me. I would watch them working out a bit first, looking particularly for my friends Bobby Ecclestone and Charlie Nolan, before going into the dressing room to change into my shoes and shorts. I used to wear black shorts with a yellow band round the waist and a yellow stripe at the side of each leg. In Warrilow's Sports Emporium they had satin boxing shorts, immaculate and colorful. Mine were home-made. Most of the time I used to skip. I loved that rope and I could do some very fancy skipping, very fast and for a very long time. Tiredness was something I'd only heard about. Then I'd box a few rounds with Charlie and Bobby, and sometimes with one of the older and more skillful boys. They were always very kind, showing me how to slip a left lead, or how to move on the ropes. I hardly ever used the heavy, shapeless punching bags; when you're thirteen years old and weigh eighty pounds it doesn't seem very necessary. Then I'd do some exercises on the mat and finish off with another burst of skipping.

Boxing with Charlie Nolan was best of all. Charlie had been in school with me, in the next desk, until he'd moved to another district. He was almost the same age and size as I was and his footwork was a miracle of economy and precision. His feet brushed the floor like a whisper as he moved perfectly about me, in a kind of smooth ritual. I, on the other hand, would jig up and down in a flashy and wasteful way, careering around the ring at top speed and not caring very much where I got to. But Charlie's hands were slow. They would sit calmly in front of him, now and again mildly exploring the space between us, and I would hit him with a variety of harmless punches that left him blinking and smiling. As he passed us, Ephraim Hamer, our trainer, would say, "Well done, Charlie!" He rarely said anything to me. After we'd showered we'd sit about listening to the bigger boys, or boasting quietly between us. Bobby Ecclestone would tell us about his work in a grocer's shop; he was errand boy in the shop where we bought our groceries and I often saw him sweeping the sawdust boards, or staggering out with huge loads to the delivery van. It was Bobby who had first brought me to the Ex-Servicemen's Club. He was fifteen and the best boxer among the boys.

One Friday evening after we had finished working out and we were sitting warm and slumped on the benches, Bobby asked me if I was going to the weigh-in the next day. I didn't even know what it was. I was always finding that there were whole areas of experience, important areas too, about which I knew nothing and other boys everything.

"Where is it?" I said carefully.

"Down at the Stadium. One o'clock," said Charlie. "I'm going."

Everything fell into place. Next day at the Stadium our local hero, Cuthbert Fletcher, who everyone said would have been featherweight champion of Wales except that he was colored, was to fight Ginger Thomas, the official champion.

"Are you going?" I asked Bobby.

"Of course," he said. "It's my dinner-time. See you outside at ten to."

All Saturday morning I hung about in a fever of anxiety in case my lunch wouldn't be ready for me in time to meet Bobby and Charlie at one o'clock outside the Stadium. But it was, and I was first there, although Charlie was not long behind me. He hadn't had his lunch and was eating a huge round of bread and jam which he'd cut for himself from a new loaf. Bobby wouldn't let us go inside the Stadium until Charlie had finished eating. A few men hung about in a corner of the empty hall, their hands deep in their overcoat pockets. They whistled softly and tunelessly and they all carried an air of vast unconcern, but when Cuthbert and Ginger Thomas appeared, they hurried forward to greet the boxers, talking excitedly to them. It was exciting too. I don't know why it should have been so, but we all felt a curious tightening of the air as the boxers smiled formally at each other. Cuthbert stepped on the scales first, and a great fat man adjusted the weights, flicking them up and down the bar with finicky little movements of his enormous fingers before he called out, in a high voice, "Eight stone and twelve pounds, gentlemen."

Cuthbert smiled, ducked his round, crinkly head at his friends, and moved away. Ginger Thomas was a lean, pale man, elegant and graceful, his mahogany hair brushed smooth and close to his head. He, too, stood on the scales and his weight was called in the fat man's brittle tenor. Everybody shook hands and at once the place was deserted.

"That's all right then," said Bobby.

"Nothing in it for weight," said Charlie.

We stood together silently, for a long time.

"Are you going to the fight?" asked Bobby.

"No," said Charlie, "my father won't let me."

Bobby looked at his shoes as they scuffed the ground in front of him, first the right shoe, then the left one.

"I can't go," he said. "Don't finish in time on Saturdays."

"I expect I'll go," I said, "if I want to."

"Will you?" said Charlie, his eyes big.

"I expect so," I said, although I knew I couldn't.

At eight that evening I was in Court Street, one of the crowd milling excitedly around the Stadium, knowing I could not get in. Slow, comfortable groups of men with money and tickets moved confidently through towards the entrance, talking with assurance about the fights they had seen in the past. On the steps near the door Trevor Bunce danced up and down, his wide, cheeky face smiling as he asked the men to take him in with them. An arrogant boy and leader of his gang, Trevor Bunce was bigger than I was. You could see him everywhere. Incredibly active, his string-colored hair hanging over his eyes, he bounced with energy through a series of escapades wherever you went. The street lights came on suddenly, and we all cheered. I knew with certainty that Trevor Bunce would get in somehow.

Now the whole road was thick with people and the few cars prodding through to outlying districts honked and revved with impatience and frustration. I moved cautiously to the pavement. I saw that, prudently, they had built a temporary barrier of corrugated sheets of metal above the low wall which separated a little yard, belonging to the Stadium, from the road. On lesser occasions many daring boys had climbed this wall—an easy feat—and run through a nest of little rooms into the hall itself. There was even a large door, always locked, which led directly into the raucous noise where even now the first of the bouts was being decided.

As I looked at the new metal sheets, Trevor Bunce threw himself past me, leapt on the wall, and, with unbelievable speed and strength, forced back the long edge of the barrier. For a moment only, it was wide enough for a boy to wriggle through and Trevor Bunce did just that. But before he was half clear, the inexorable metal wall snapped back, pinning him at the waist, his legs kicking wildly; and even as we looked, we heard clearly and without mistake, a sound as of a dry stick breaking. Then Trevor Bunce began to scream.

In seconds, it seems to me now, we had ripped away the corrugated wall and its wooden framework, and men's gentle arms carried Trevor away. I saw him as he went, his face white and wet, but his eyes were open. He cradled his right forearm carefully, because it was broken.

By this time many of us were in the yard itself, aimlessly stacking the six-foot sheets of tin in an untidy heap near the wall. There must have been forty or fifty of us; boys, young workless men, and a few older men who were there by chance, it seemed. Yet, haphazard and leaderless as we were, we suddenly lifted our restive heads and, like some swollen river, streamed for the door that led to the Stadium's lesser rooms.

I didn't want to go with them. Some shred of caution tried hard to hold me back, but my treacherous legs hurried me on, gasping. We met nobody, except in a corridor an old man wiping saucers with a wet cloth. He pressed himself against the wall, his mouth wide open, and we were past him before he got a word out. And then we were in the great hall itself, our force broken against the huge weight of the legal customers. We lost ourselves among them at once.

The noise, the heat, the immense, expectant good humor made the whole place intoxicating, but I could see nothing except, high overhead, a blue, unshifting cloud of cigarette smoke. Agile though I was, I could not push or wriggle another inch nearer the ring. It was Freddie Benders who came to my help. Freddie didn't fight much, because he was nearly thirty years old. His ears were rubbery and he had few teeth, but he often came down to the club and sometimes he'd let us spar with him. You could hit him with everything you had, right on the chin even, and he'd only laugh.

When he saw me he shouted out, "Make room for the boy there, let the boy get down to the front."

Grumbling and laughing, the men inched more closely together and I squeezed my way almost to the ringside.

"That's right," shouted Freddie. "That boy is going to make a good 'un. Keep your eyes on Cuthbert tonight, boy!"

I saw the fight. I saw every moment of the fifteen rounds, and it was a great fight, I know it was. Yet all the time it was on, all the time incisive Ginger Thomas moved forward with a speed and viciousness I had not imagined, what I really saw was Trevor Bunce's white face, what I heard was the stark snapping of his bones. When the fighters moved around the ring, the crowd was silent and absorbed and at the end of each round there was a great sigh before they clapped and shouted. I think Ginger Thomas won, but at the end the referee held Cuthbert's arm up and we all cheered, with relief and pride rather than with certainty. Ginger Thomas stood in the center of the ring, aloof and unmoved; his pale eyes glittered in the arc-lights, and then he turned and swaggered easily away. His lack of emotion disturbed me more than the terrible, precise fury and venom of his attacks.

When I got home my parents had nothing to say to me. I was so late, my crime was so enormous, that all they could do was to point to the stairs; I hurried up to my room to shiver gratefully under the icy sheets. I knew I should never sleep again and, even as I realized this, fell at once to sleep. When I awoke all was dark and confusing, and my right forearm was throbbing with pain. Struggling with darkness, I found the fingers of my left hand tight in a cramping grip around my right arm. The pain made me think of poor Trevor Bunce, in hospital surely, and I felt with quick relief the whole, frail bones in my own arms.

The following Tuesday I was late getting to the Club, but

only because I had found my French homework particularly difficult. I waved to the boys, changed eagerly, and soon had the old skipping-rope humming away. Everything began to feel fine. It wasn't until I put the gloves on to spar with Charlie Nolan that I realized that something was wrong. I kept on seeing Ginger Thomas, destructive and graceful, his hands cocked, moving into Cuthbert, as he had on the Saturday night. I could see his face, relaxed and faintly curious, the sudden blur as he released three or four short punches before sliding away. I knew too that I was doing this to Charlie, but I couldn't stop. Charlie was bleeding from the mouth and nose and he was pawing away with his gloves open. I could tell he was frightened. Yet I kept on ripping punches at him, my hands suddenly hard and urgent and the huge, muffling gloves we used no longer clumsy. I could hear Mr. Hamer shouting as Charlie hid in a corner and then somebody had me round the waist, throwing me almost across the ring. Charlie was crying, but in a little while Bobby Ecclestone put an arm round Charlie's shoulders, talking to him softly. Nobody said anything to me and I sat on the bench. I thought I was quivering all over, but when I looked at my legs they were all right. I felt as if I were going to be sick. Nothing seemed to matter very much. I walked to the dressing room and began to change. I was so tired that it was an effort to take off my ring clothes, and when I pulled my vest over my head I could feel my face wet with my own tears. I took a good look at the room before I went out, then I shut the door behind me, very quietly. It sounded just as it always had, the slithering of the shoes around the ball or the heavy bag, the rhythmical slapping of the rope on the boards as somebody did some lively skipping.

Nobody saw me go. As I went down the stairs I could see through the window little groups of quiet drinkers in the room below, but they could not see me in the dark passage.

I never went back there. Sometimes when I went for groceries, some cheese maybe, or some canned stuff, I would see Bobby Ecclestone in the shop. He didn't say anything to me and I didn't say anything to him. It was as if we had never been friends.

A House Divided

I'm glad I had my boyhood before the war, before the '39 war, that is. I'm glad I knew the world when it was innocent and golden and that I grew up in a tiny country whose borders had been trampled over so often that they had been meaningless for centuries. My home was in a mining town fast growing derelict, in Wales, and the invincible scrawny grass and scrubby birch trees were beginning to cover the industrial rubbish that lay in heaps about us.

It all seemed very beautiful to me, the small, tottering cottages in peeling rows on the hillside, the pyramids of black spoil that lay untidily above them, the rivers thick as velvet where the brown trout were beginning to appear again. But I read in a book that our river had once been famous for its salmon and that the last great silver fish had been caught there in 1880, and I knew that there had been a more complete perfection, a greener Eden.

Further west was such a green county, Carmarthenshire. When I was eleven years old, I was put on a bus for Carmarthen town, there to meet my aunt with whom I was to stay for a whole summer month, and it was then that I entered into my kingdom. My aunt met me at the coach station and we got into a smaller bus, full to its racks with people, parcels, chickens, bundles of newspapers, two sheep dogs. I had never seen grass so ablaze with emerald, nor a river so wide and jocund as the Towy. The bus was full of the quick Welsh language of which I didn't know a word, so I sat warily on the hard edge of my seat, observing from

the rims and corners of my eyes. My aunt said nothing to
me.

Groaning brokenly, the bus hauled up the hills north of
the town, lurching to an occasional amiable halt in the
centers of villages, outside the doors of simple inns, at deserted crossroads high on the moors. Through its hot, moving windows I saw small white farmhouses appear, one
after the other, each at the heart of an aimless cluster of irregular fields. I knew I would sleep that night in such a
house. I had never been away before, not even for one
night. I looked at my silent and terrible aunt. She grinned
suddenly, dug me ferociously in the ribs, and gave me a
round, white peppermint. Comforted, I worked my tongue
around the hot sweet. It was going to be all right.

We had reached the flat top of the mountain and the little
bus throbbed doggedly along an uncompromisingly straight
road. Then we began to drop, running through sweeping
shallow bends that took us lower and lower into a valley of
unbelievable lushness. As the nose of the bus turned this
way and that, I caught glimpses of a superb river, rich and
wide, its brilliant surface paler than the sky it reflected. My
aunt and I got off at the river bridge. The stone parapets
were built in little triangular bays. You could wait in them
while traffic passed. My aunt and I did this, and I looked
down into the water, relishing its music, its cold clarity
dappled over stones.

We had perhaps half a mile to walk, the road turning
from the river as it swung south, and then we took a farm
track back in the direction of the water. We passed but one
house all the time we walked and that was a small, one-
storied cottage with a low door and three windows set in its
front. An old woman sat straight-backed on a wooden settle
outside the door. She was shelling peas, placing the pale
green ovals as if they were pearls into a china basin held on
her lap, letting the empty pods fall into a bucket. She didn't
stop doing this all the time she was talking to my aunt. Her
long dress, made of some hard material, had been worn and

washed to a faded blue. At her throat was a gold brooch which said "Mother."

"That's Mrs. Lewis," said my aunt. "A tough old bird, she is."

I looked back at Mrs. Lewis, upright and purposeful outside her front door in the evening sunlight.

"Is she very old then?" I asked.

"Not so old," my aunt said. "Over sixty though, I expect. She used to work the farm next to us until last year. Worked it on her own, she did. Now she lets it to her nephew, Emrys. You'll see him about—his farm is on the river side of this lane and ours down here, on the right."

My case began to get heavy, so I hoisted it onto my shoulder.

Not long afterward we turned off the lane and followed a little stream which took us to the house, where my uncle was waiting.

I can't remember what else happened that day, but the pattern of following days is clear in my mind. Every morning I'd get up reasonably early, wash, and go downstairs to the kitchen. My uncle, a plump, voluble man, would begin talking as soon as he heard my foot on the stairs, and was already launched into some wild tale when I got into the room. He would be stretching up, on the tips of his small feet, to cut rashers from the side of bacon which hung from the beamed ceiling. The knife he used was large, black-handled, and sharp as fright. The bacon, pallid with fat, had two streaks of lean meat running meanly through it, and it swung about as he cut, but years of practice allowed my uncle to carve a slice as uniformly thin as if it had been done by machine. The frying pan, and the kettle too for that matter, hung from hooks above the enormous fire. My uncle always cooked my breakfast. He would take three of the yellow rashers and place them gently in the iron pan, adding, when the fat had begun to run, a thick slice of bread.

Then he'd crack an egg and put that in. It was delicious.
The bacon, crisp and dry, broke beneath my knife; the
bread, fried brown on the outside, was succulent and full as
a sponge with warm fat. Every morning my uncle would
put my plate before me with a mild pride. He never
stopped talking to me. He stood in front of his fire, his
thumbs in his pockets, rocking gently forward and backward on his tiny feet, his eyes opening wide when he
reached the climax of some innocent tale. When I'd finished
my food he would go off to the fields, there to work with
furious, haphazard energy. He had always finished, apart
from the evening milking, by early afternoon.

Sometimes I worked with him and he liked this. But more
often I would wander away on some inconclusive ploy of
my own. Once I tracked the source of the little stream which
supplied all our water at the farm, and which had never run
dry, they said, even in the hottest summers. It started less
than a mile away, in the foothills, a small, round pool filled
by three bubbling heads of water. I stayed almost a whole
morning, lying on the grass, watching the water burst
through a fine white sand, grains of which were carried up
and away in an erratic dance. After a time I began to see
that there was a kind of regularity in the way the springs
gushed up, a kind of pattern. I told my uncle about the
springs. He had never been there, but my aunt said she
went once a year to clear it of leaves. There were no trees
near it. I think she used to go there just to see the sand
dancing.

By this time I'd met Emrys Hughes, Mrs. Lewis' nephew
and our neighbor, so I thought I was entitled to walk over
his land, too. The first time I did this I saw Emrys standing
beside his dairy. I waved to him, but he didn't wave back.
He stood there a moment as if confused, then he turned and
dived out of sight. I told my aunt and uncle about this.

"Oh, he's very shy, is Emrys," my uncle said. "You
needn't worry about that. He don't mind you being on his
land, not at all. He'd *like* you to go over."

My aunt sniffed gently.

"Emrys is very nice," she said, "very helpful."

She thought deeply and then gave her judgment.

"Yes, very nice," she said delicately, "but not quite the round penny, if you know what I mean."

I thought of Emrys, of his long awkward body and innocent, gentle face, of his habit of ducking his head at meaningless moments. I could see what she meant.

"Oh, he's all right," said my uncle stoutly. "He's his father all over again, and old Dafydd Hughes never did a mite of harm to anybody."

So I continued to walk through Emrys' fields and after a while he waved back at me and even spoke to me. He had very little English and our conversation was simple and limited. Mostly we'd stand and beam at each other. His wife was more talkative altogether, and I got into the habit of calling at their house about midmorning. We used to drink tea, the three of us, out of large Victorian cups, and eat a great many of the round flat cakes full of currants that were baked on a thick iron plate directly above the open fire. I used to read the local paper to Emrys and his wife. It didn't occur to me until much later that they couldn't read. They were both about twenty-three when first I went to stay with my aunt.

Emrys' farm had one great advantage over ours; it was bordered on the west by the miraculous river. What I liked to do was to have my breakfast, do a few jobs about the farm, and then go over to Emrys'. I'd read to them, or we'd hold one of our slow, repetitive conversations, and then, very gently and by a roundabout route so that I would enjoy the going, I'd go down to the river. But one morning I awoke particularly early, startling my uncle, who was alone in the kitchen, singing and cooking his own breakfast.

"Good God, boy!" he said. "What's the matter? Can't you sleep?"

We had our food together and I went straight out into the early world. I had never known that such pure light existed and I was suddenly and overwhelmingly filled with a wish to see the river. I ran through Emrys' fields toward the water, and even some distance off I could see the man on the far bank, staggering slightly and hauling away at his fishing rod. When I arrived at the bank, gasping, I could see he'd got into something big, his rod bent in a deep arc from the butt, held in his gripping hands, to the tip which was only inches above the water. I couldn't see the line, even when he heaved sturdily back before winding in. He was not a young man and he wore a clergyman's collar.

"I wish you were over here," he called. "I've been half an hour with this one, and I could do with some help."

I ran for the bridge, over it, and down the other bank, splashing through stony shallows most of the way. But it took me seven or eight minutes and by the time I'd got down to the old boy he'd landed his fish. I'd never seen anything so enormous, nor so beautiful. I spoke for some time to the old man, but apart from the fact that he was on a fishing holiday and that he lived in the Midlands, I can remember nothing of him. I can remember everything about the salmon. I could take you now, at this moment, to the place where I first saw him lying hugely in the grass, his great head up against a clump of dock. I know the gradations of his color, the position of his every scale. A trickle of blood came over his lower jaw.

"A fresh-run fish," the old man said.

I didn't know what he meant, but I knew that I soon would. I went home in a daze. I was caught, all right.

It was easier than I had imagined. Both my uncle and aunt thought it entirely natural that I should want to catch salmon.

"Where's that old rod of mine, Marged?" asked my uncle. "The boy can begin with that. I'll get him a license when I call into town. Don't forget, boy, the river is dangerous, you'll have to learn it like a book. And have a word with Emrys—he's a marvel with fish, is Emrys."

He was, too. Boys learn a great deal by imitation, and I

learned by imitating Emrys. He knew where every salmon in the river was to be found; he could point out places where legendary fish of the past had been caught by his father or his uncle. I was killing biggish fish right from the beginning, most of them with an old two-piece greenheart that Emrys had used when he was a boy. He had a box full of tied flies, lures of an entirely local pattern that I've never seen anywhere else, although I've caught fish all over the world since. I still have them, the old greenheart and Emrys' box of flies. I've not used either of them since 1948, when I bought the first of my split-cane rods. When my month was up I didn't want to go home.

My uncle jollied me along.

"Time you went," he said. "The boys in the Cerys Arms are complaining that there won't be a fish in the river unless we send you home soon."

He loaded me with gifts, shook hands as if we had been friends for fifty years, and told me to come back at Easter.

"March," he said. "That's when the season begins. We'll be waiting for you."

So year after year I spent my springs and summers in that fertile and timeless place. I'd go into town the day after my arrival. I'd go into Mr. Protheroe's shop and buy my river license. Mr. Protheroe would tell me what fish had been caught already and I'd inspect his new stock of tackle. Then it was off to the water. Although Emrys came with me less often than on my early visits, we always had at least five or six long days together. We did some night-fishing, too, after sea trout. The river was unbelievably busy then, its noises louder and more mysterious than in secure daylight, its cool air hawked by bats and soft-flying owls.

The summer of '39 was long and hot, and the river had fallen sadly below fishing level. One Sunday morning Emrys and I were out on the water, fishing for memories mostly. We sat on the bank, throwing a line now and then

over runs where we'd caught good fish in other years. The
water was warm and stale, and we knew it was no good
hoping for anything. The little salmon parr, little finger-
lings, sidled lazily in the shallows. We saw my uncle come
slowly through the fields, head bowed under the sun.

"Daro!" said Emrys. "It must be hot to make your uncle
walk slow like that."

But it wasn't the heat. He had come to tell us that war had
been declared. We didn't say much about it. We walked
back to the house and I packed my case and tackle,
mounted the old Rudge Whitworth motorcycle I owned at
the time, and rode home. I knew that the world of summer
fishing had come to an end. It was time for me to go else-
where. Within a year I was in the Army.

My uncle wrote to me once a fortnight, on Sundays. His
careful letters, the narrow, upright script, kept me informed
of all his artless news. I learned that old Mrs. Lewis had suf-
fered a stroke and was bedridden, that Emrys and his wife
had left the farm to live with her. The local lawyer, Lemuel
Evans, had found a tenant for the farm until such time as
Emrys could return.

Later, Emrys was called up. I couldn't imagine him in the
Army. He was thirty years old then, and more naïve than
most children. In the intervals of keeping myself out of the
more senseless military activities, I sometimes thought of
Emrys. I needn't have worried. Unable to read, his English
an almost unintelligible dialect, he was of little value to the
Army. He was sent home after serving for three months.

In the spring of 1944 I had some embarkation leave and I
spent a week of it at the farm. There was nobody at home
when I arrived—it was market day at Cardigan—but the
door was never locked in that house. I went inside, dumped
my case, got my rod out, and tackled up. I thought I could
get half an hour in before my aunt and uncle returned, and I
walked through the familiar fields of what had been Emrys'
farm, savoring every moment. When I got to the water I
unhooked my fly from the cork butt and got some line out

ready to cast. The water looked right, a lot of it and a beautiful clear brown, the color of the peat bogs it came from. I gave my rod a flick or two, just to clear my wrist, then threw a long cast across the pool. Someone shouted behind me, but I took my time, keeping the line nice and tight until I was ready to reel in. Then I looked around.

He was a thickset man, dark and hard, in his late thirties. I smiled at him.

"What do you think you're doing?" he said.

I told him who I was.

"I know who you are," he said. "You have no more right to fish my water than anyone else."

I explained that both Emrys and Mrs. Lewis had always allowed me to fish there, but I could see it was useless. I didn't want trouble and he looked strong enough for caution. Holding my rod above my head, I walked out of his farmyard and up the lane. I thought of calling at Mrs. Lewis' cottage to complain to her or to Emrys, but there was a little car outside the door when I reached the house, so I walked on. I crossed the bridge over the river, climbed the stile, and moved down the opposite bank. I could see my uncle's surly neighbor standing where I'd left him. I stood with the width of the river between us, and cast in. I've never been a stylish angler; effective, perhaps, but never stylish. But that cast was perfect. I put the fly down as effortlessly as it could be done, the line unrolling smoothly forward on the unblemished surface, the lure falling as naturally as thistledown. It was taken at once, as I knew it would be, and I landed the fish after fifteen minutes. It was the biggest fish I'd ever caught and I still haven't equalled it. Just over eighteen pounds it went, and I cast for it, hooked it, and landed it under the furious, silent gaze of the man on the other side of the river. It was very satisfying. After I'd pulled it out I went lower down and caught two more, both over twelve pounds. I wasn't out more than a couple of hours altogether, and then I waded across downstream, just above an old woollen mill where Emrys and I sometimes fished, and walked back across the fields to my uncle's house. After supper I told my people about their neighbor's boorish behavior.

"We don't have much to do with him," said my uncle.

He looked uncomfortable and ashamed.

"He's not a nice man, do you see," my aunt said, "not like poor Emrys."

I could see they didn't want to talk about him, so I said no more. Emrys and his wife came in shortly after. They were pleased and excited. We had a merry evening, but Emrys would say nothing about his three months in the Army, however closely I pressed him.

"I didn't like it there," he said. "It was terrible in the Army."

"Lemuel Evans came to see the aunt today," said Mrs. Hughes. "She signed the will. Left everything to Emrys she has, the cottage, the farm, everything. Mr. Evans read it out to us, then the aunt signed the will, two copies, then Emrys and me."

"Why should you sign it?" asked my uncle.

"We are the witnesses," said Mrs. Hughes. "Emrys has always been able to sign his name, although he's no scholar, of course."

"Stands to reason I'd have to sign it," said Emrys. "All the money comes to me, doesn't it?"

"I'm very glad," my aunt said. "Let's hope that Mrs. Lewis has many years of happy life in front of her and that when her time comes nothing goes wrong to spoil what is to come to you. You've been very good to her, the two of you."

When they'd gone I spoke to my uncle about the will. I thought it unlikely that beneficiaries could witness a will they would eventually gain from.

"Say nothing," said my uncle cautiously. "Don't get involved in it. We are no match for the lawyers."

I looked at him and saw with compassion that he had grown old. His talk, that bubbling mixture of innocent wild tales, chuckles, exclamations of surprise and delight, now held long silences also. Sometimes I caught him with a strange look in his eyes, as if he were measuring long distances. He died when I was abroad and my aunt lived only a few years after him.

After the war I didn't go back there. There seemed no reason for it, although I often went down into Pembrokeshire. Last month, though, I took the mid-Wales route and found myself again on that old river bridge. I left the car at the head of the lane and walked down. It seemed unchanged, but Mrs. Lewis' cottage was empty and unkempt, its windows covered by an untidy lace of cobwebs and fine dirt. I started to go on to the farm, but couldn't face it now that my people were dead and strangers lived there. I pushed my way through hawthorn and nettle into Mrs. Lewis' garden. The apple trees, mossed to the twigs, were covered with the hard red apples I remembered so well. There were greenfinches in the hedge, marvellous birds. I walked around the cottage, remembering. The roof looked sound and dry, the walls sturdy. You can often buy such a cottage for surprisingly little. I could use it for weekends and fish these waters again.

I drove back into town and went into Mr. Protheroe's shop, walking into the back room as I'd always done. He was sitting there, white-haired and frail, but quite recognizably the man who had sold me so many bits and pieces of my youth. He had a box of flies in front of him. Mallard and claret they were, beautiful flies. I bought a dozen and then I told him who I was. It was heartwarming to be remembered.

"Come down for some fishing?" he asked.

I told him that my interest was rather different, that I had seen old Mrs. Lewis' cottage and thought of buying it. He was pleased.

"You ought to come back," he said. "There have always been members of your family hereabouts. I went to school with your uncles."

"We haven't been here for twenty-five years," I said.

"That's not long when we're talking of families," he said. "Old Mrs. Lewis' cottage now. It could look very nice with a bit of paint here and there and a good cleanup. Nobody's lived there since she died, or a few months after. Lemuel Evans is the man for you to see. His office is just up the street, next to the Post Office."

"I expect Emrys Hughes went back to the farm," I said.

"Well, no," said old Protheroe. "There was a big shock over that. When Mrs. Lewis died and the will was proved, it turned out that she'd left every mortal thing to Lemuel Evans. The farm, the cottage, every mortal thing. There was a lot of talk, of course."

He looked out of his window at the orderly garden.

"Nobody could prove anything," he said.

"What happened to Emrys?" I asked.

"He took it hard," said Mr. Protheroe. "He let it get on top of him, and he never was, as you know, a man quick to understanding. I see him from time to time, but he's not good for much now. No, not for much. Talks to himself and so on."

"Not a very nice story," I said.

"Nothing in this world is perfect," said the old man. "Don't let it bother you. Go up now and have a word with Lemuel Evans. Tell him I sent you and let him know who you are."

I went up to Lemuel Evans' office and was shown into a dirty room, the lower half of its windows covered by screens of rusty gauze the color of liver. There was dust everywhere. A few box files, sagging and empty, stood on a shelf. Evans was there, a tall old man so dry and sapless he seemed made of tinder. A great plume of white hair swept off his forehead. I asked him about the cottage.

He nodded slowly.

"It's a nice little property," he said. His voice was astonishingly vigorous. "A pleasant situation, and very sound. How much would you be thinking of paying for it?"

I told him that there was a lot to be done to the house before anyone could think of living in it and I offered him a silly amount, really silly.

His answer surprised me.

"It will certainly need some renovation," he said, "and it will only deteriorate if left empty. I think we can do business at the figure you mention."

I said I'd think about it and let him know. I couldn't get poor Emrys out of my mind. I thought I might buy the cottage and give it back to Emrys; I thought I ought to ask Evans outright why he had cheated my old friend. I realized I was shaking with anger. I walked out, Lemuel Evans following me to the door.

I went back down the hill toward Protheroe's shop. He was standing outside, waiting for me.

"You won't be buying the house," he said.

"No," I said.

"You aren't the first," he said. "No, not the first, by a long way."

I didn't say anything. I was suddenly indifferent to everything.

"Come inside and have some tea," old Protheroe said.

"I haven't time now," I said.

I got in the car and drove away. It began to rain as I crossed the river bridge and by the time I'd climbed the hill a persistent soft rain drove in at me. I stopped the car and looked back. The town was hidden by falling rain, its roofs, its bridge, the little outlying cottages, but to the south, the way I was going, the river shone in its valley like an enormous snail track.

Three Shots for Charlie Betson

We moved into this village fifteen years ago, a week before Christmas. Our furniture was taken away in the early morning and we had followed by leisurely train after lunch. It was already dark when we reached Brighton and it was bitterly cold. We got on the bus which was to take us to our new house and we were the only passengers. A wind off the bleak sea came unchecked through the body of the coach and we sat huddled against fatigue and numbing cold in the faulty havens of our greatcoats. It took an hour and a half to reach the village, a distance of only twelve miles.

I couldn't find the key when we arrived at the house, but the back door was open and we tumbled in, regretting that we'd ever heard of the place. But a huge fire was burning in the grate, a loaf of bread and two bottles of milk stood on the kitchen table, and soon we began to recognize our nomadic furniture in its strange corners. I found the key in a briefcase I'd carried with me. I opened the front door and there on the step was a cabbage, a bag of potatoes, and a bunch of mimosa. I couldn't see anyone about and there wasn't a sound. In those days the village street had no lighting and we had no very near neighbors. The school building opposite was merely a dark bulk against a dark sky.

I picked up the vegetables and the mimosa and carried them in to my wife. She was enchanted, warmed by anonymous generosity. We reinforced our hot milk with big slugs of whiskey, made toast by the lovely fire, and went happy to bed. We talked before sleep of the people who had so tactfully welcomed us, because we knew nobody in the village.

Old Bill Francis had done it all himself, trudging sturdily over the three fields between our house and his, but I didn't know that until months later.

The next morning was full of rain and we worked away indoors, eating a sketchy meal about midday. Afterwards, in a break in the rain, I dressed against the weather and went out. I found a cinder path running between two high thorn hedges. It led to a lane very little wider than itself, but properly surfaced and serving a scatter of small houses along its length. A sign called it Crook Lane.

I still hadn't seen anyone since our arrival in the place and it was a relief to find a man trying to prop open a field gate with a fallen branch.

"Here," said the man. "You've come just in time. Hold the gate open while I drive these cows across the lane and into this other field of mine."

He was a huge old man, his large red face carrying an ample nose. I held the gate and he drove his three amicable heifers across the road and into his other field. The old man was lame, one leg deformed, stiff at the bent knee joint. He came up to me as I closed the gate, looking at me for a long time. He was inspecting me, his expression cheerful and sardonic, his little blue eyes alight and curious.

"Them cows," he said, "they can be real cantankerous, so you came in very handy. Just come to live here, have you?"

I said I had. I pointed across the fields to the roof of my house. It was the first house we'd ever owned.

"Saw your lights come on," said the old man, "last night. You won't stay long, you won't like it here. We're a close lot in this village, keep ourselves to ourselves. No, you won't find it easy in this village, I can tell you. We don't take to strangers."

He was Bill Francis, and he smiled at me with enormous friendship and satisfaction.

"Come down the house," he said, "and have a cup of tea."

He jerked his head towards our house.

"My father used to live in that one," he said, "that house of yours. Pretty as a picture it used to be."

"You'll have hard work of it," he said sternly, "if you want that house to look as it did in my father's day."

We walked together down Crook Lane towards his house. He told me that his brother was a retired sergeant of police, that he himself had over three thousand pounds in the bank, that he had been very fond of boxing when he was young.

"I loved it, I did," he said. His great wide laughter rang in the empty lane. "I liked nothing better of a Sunday morning than to get the gloves on with a good boy and to belt ourselves tired. Many's the time I've come home with my face swollen up twice its size."

He shook his large head sadly.

"My wife didn't like it though," he said. "She didn't like it, and in the end I gave it up. She's been dead now these five years, a lovely woman she was."

Bill Francis' garden was a delight. Although it was winter, there was about it an air of plenty: it seemed merely awaiting some signal to blossom into miraculous fecundity. It was an artist's garden, not only immaculately neat, but its proportions were immediately satisfying, the branches of his apple trees pruned so that they made clear and perfect shapes in the air, the patterns of his flower beds coherent and full of interest. Bill's house was the same, the furniture good and glowingly cared for. The cups we drank from were old, fragile, very beautiful.

It became a habit for me to walk across the cinder path in the afternoons, unless I was into something very important, to hold open old Bill's gate and walk on down to have a cup of tea with him. Years later, when he was in his eighties and grown frail, I used to go over and see to his heifers myself. He always had two or three running on, to sell when they were down-calving. I liked him.

It was inevitable that I should have come across the Betsons sooner or later, for they were so large a family that ev-

eryone in the village was in some way or another connected
with them. Physically, too, they were so positive and vigorous that it would have been impossible to ignore them. I'd
seen the children, without knowing who they were, on
their way to school. They walked up the road as far as my
garden wall, silent, tall boys, very fair and upright, and
crossed over the road there. There must have been half a
dozen of them—in fact, there were seven, and now that I
put my mind to it I can give a name to every one of them.
They never laughed or played and they ranged between six
years old and fifteen.

A busy main road ran the straggling length of the village
and I was often anxious about the safety of children as they
went to and from the school, but not the Betsons. Casually
and with dignity they walked, crossing the road when it
was absolutely clear. The youngest boys were the children
of the two Betson sisters, but I didn't know that. None of
them spoke to me, nor did they show they were aware of
me as I began, in the drier afternoons, to set my garden to
rights. Lord, how they must have laughed in the village as I
cut, tore, and burned. I killed a long bank of Albertine
roses, the pride of the garden, through pure ignorance.

Occasionally, if it were too cold for digging, or if I were
thinking of something, I'd cut through the school playground and over a couple of fields. A small river ran
through a shallow valley there, and the light was so clear it
gave the heart a lift even on intransigent days. Often, wild
duck flew honking over the water, or landed noisily, feath-
ering the surface with their braced feet. It's all built over
now. Everything changes.

One afternoon I walked through the school fields as the
older boys were playing football. I'd not long given up playing myself, had played for good clubs. I walked through the
intent boys as a high ball came upfield in an inviting parab-
ola, made entirely for me. I was rising to it in an instinct of
joy, neck and shoulders taut, knowing my forehead would
meet the ball perfectly. Out of the corner of my eye I saw

someone come up with me, and I turned slightly so that my shoulder would smother our impact. Even so he almost got to the ball before me. Amused and ashamed, I challenged more fiercely than was at all necessary. Hell, I wasn't even supposed to be playing. But the boy dropped cleverly away, landing easily and breaking at once into his stride. He was the biggest of the fair Betson boys I'd seen; he was Charlie Betson.

Hodges, the schoolmaster, came over, a round, gentle, smiling man, the most comfortable-looking man I've ever known. When I think of him now I see his dark, smooth face and imagine him with a pipe in his mouth. In reality, he didn't smoke at all. I got to know him well before he moved away to a bigger school in Lancashire. He's dead now, died unnecessarily in a stupid car smash, in fog, about three years back.

"That was nicely done," he said. "I wish I were able to get up like that, but I was never a games player."

I grinned at him. He was about my own age, couldn't have been much more.

"I hope you didn't mind," I said. "I'm just passing through to the river."

"No trouble," he said. "It's a public footpath anyway."

I walked on and was climbing the stile when he called me.

It turned out that he was the only man on the staff of that small school, his colleagues being two elderly ladies who taught the younger children, and he felt the boys were not getting the games coaching he would have liked. In the end I said I'd go across once a week and take the bigger boys for football. I did it for almost ten years. It helped to keep me fit and I used to enjoy showing off. Old Bill Francis, who was on the school committee, was delighted with me.

I've never seen another boy with such quick and accurate reflexes as Charlie Betson. He was already taller than I am, but very thin, as some adolescent boys are. He could kick a ball with either foot without thinking, he could catch marvellously well. I thought I had found a great player in the making, but it was all physical. He hadn't an idea in his head. It took me some time to realize this, since Charlie was so shy he didn't speak to me. I talked to Hodges about him.

"The Betsons are all the same," he said. "I've had dozens of them in the school, and Charlie is the archetypal Betson. Beautiful to look at, quiet, and hard-working, but stupid. Charlie, for example, can't read at all. He's had special tuition for years, but he gets nowhere."

Not long after this I was in my garden when Charlie looked over the wall. I asked him in. In about two minutes it became obvious that Charlie knew more about gardening than I ever would. He came to work for me on Saturday mornings and I taught him to read out of seed catalogues.

Spring comes early to this part of the country and it was particularly lovely that year, the first year we lived in the village. Towards the end of April, the sun already warm, cuckoos shouting, I was in Crook Lane talking to Bill Francis. It was Sunday, and the church bells were floating their traditional messages over the fields. My wife's birthday was that day, and I'd mentioned this to Bill some days earlier.

"Why, that'll be Primrose Sunday, look," he'd said, "a good day for a birthday."

I had only laughed, but that morning we had found a small bunch of primroses on the doorstep, in an exquisite tiny jug. Afterwards he never forgot her birthday, never failed to leave her such a gift. We have the jugs still. We used to find it very moving, imagining his enormous hands plucking with such delicacy among the threadlike stalks of the flowers, placing them artfully with a few of their puckered leaves in the little jugs. I'd gone over to tell Bill of her delight and we carried on talking in the renewing warmth.

But something drew Bill's attention as we spoke. He looked down the lane, an expression at once stern, surprised, and disapproving on his face. I turned to see what could have caused this. A strange little procession was moving towards us, ceremonious, quiet, celebrating ritually, it seemed, the spring of the year.

A group of young Betsons, tall and silent, were walking up the lane towards us, the smaller boys forming the erratic edges of the party. The older fellows, those who were at work and whom I had not seen before, were carrying on their shoulders a simple throne, adapted from a wooden armchair. Chestnut poles were fastened to clamps on each side of the chair, and the young men held the poles on their strong shoulders, their identical golden heads tilted away. They walked in unison, easily, unconcernedly. There was something noble in the way they walked; theirs was a willing submission.

Seated up in the chair, a plaid blanket neatly over his knees, was an old man. Up high there, his head above the uncut hedges, he had accepted his elevation as entirely natural. He wore an old hat, and a thick scarf, its ends tucked into his coat, was crossed over his chest. As he passed us, the old man lifted a hand in greeting. He was completely at ease, relaxed as if he were sitting at his own fireside. He smiled directly at Bill Francis and his smile was full and subtle, as amused and meaningful as an hour of speech.

"Bill," he said.

His voice was deep, gentle, and mocking. Bill Francis stood unmoving at my side, the corners of his mouth pulled down and his face stony. He nodded once, a brisk, hard butt of the head, in response to the old man's greeting. The old man was very ill. Long gray hair hung below his hat and lay on his pale cheeks. The skin of his face was thick and coarse, pitted and lumped like the skin of an orange. He was obviously the father of the tribe, the patriarchal Betson. Nobody else said a word, not even Charlie. As they passed us, Charlie took his place among the bearers, moving in to relieve one of his brothers. I could feel his eyes slide remotely away from me. Behind the men two or three little girls quarrelled and scrambled along. These were the old man's granddaughters. I only knew one of his daughters and that was Sarah Betson, a great slashing creature tall as an Amazon, two or three years older than Charlie. She moved away to London when she was nineteen, came home at Christmas for a few years, and walked through the village in her vivid clothes before disappearing from our lives forever. Facially she was very like Charlie, but bolder and more confident.

We watched Mr. Betson and his splendid phalanx around the bend in the lane. He turned once and waved a hand from his dipping throne as he went, and old Bill Francis breathed deeply through his nose.

"Them owdacious Betsons," he said, his disapproval palpable. "There always have been Betsons in this village, and by the look of it there always will be."

I thought it admirable that his sons should take the sick old man out in his carried chair in the first good sun of the year, and I said so. I was shocked at Bill Francis' anger. He turned on me, fairly hissing, white spittle on his lower lip, two hectic lights on his cheekbones.

"You ain't been here long enough to know anything," he said, "and you ain't got enough sense to look about you. While the Betsons increase and flourish, what's happening to the decent people, eh? What's to happen to the decent people, just think of that!"

He wheeled like a great ship of state and marched solemnly away. He didn't ask me down to his house. That was the only time we ever approached a disagreement.

In the summer Mr. Betson died, in great agony. Charlie left school and went to work on one of the farms. I didn't see him often, and when I did it would be on a Saturday, or on some holiday, when he'd be dressed in his finery. He grew rapidly. Tall when I first knew him, he was well over six feet by the time he was seventeen, and he walked like a guardsman. Colonel Fletcher gave Charlie one of his labradors. Sometimes I'd see him at a distance, walking one of the hedges with his dog, a gun under his arm. He was great on rabbits, was Charlie, fast, cool, invariably accurate.

One Friday afternoon I heard a frightening scream of brakes outside the house. I was in the kitchen. I put down a cup so slowly and carefully that I was driven to anger by my cautious body, ánd then I ran outside. Two little girls were clinging together against the wall, their voices inhumanly high as they shrieked. A truck, heavily loaded with timber, was stopped halfway across the road, its front wheels wrenched at a despairing angle, and a little brown dog lay near the off-side wheel. It was pitifully broken, blood and fragments of bone everywhere, but it was still alive. I knew the little girls. They were sisters who lived higher up the village, and they owned the dog. I ran towards them, not knowing what to do, and held them in my arms. The young driver was getting out of his cab. He was white and shaking, his mouth opening and shutting without words. Everything seemed to be happening slowly and with a dreadful clarity. I could see Charlie Betson leaping over the gate on the other side of the road, landing lightly, his face expressionless and remote.

"Take the little girls away," he said to me. "Take them into your house. I'll see to this."

As we went inside I heard the crack of Charlie's gun, but I don't think the girls did. Children are remarkable, so resilient. Those little girls were shocked and genuinely heartbroken and they sobbed for an hour, but afterwards they ate a good meal with us and afterwards we played a riotous game of cards before we took them home. The road was clean, all evidence of the small tragedy washed and swept away. The kids' parents were out, I remember, and we had to leave them with a neighbor. I've not thought of it for years. It happened the year Bill Francis took to his bed and I became a member of the Parish Council in his place.

Charlie moved from the village when he got married. His wife came from a little place about ten miles away and they found a house there. I saw them together once or twice, Charlie and his wife, and they looked marvellous. She was a tall girl, athletic and fair, with an open, smiling face, a generous face. They had two children quite quickly. I was amused to think of Charlie suddenly so mature and responsible. Time goes, of course; I had not seen the sudden quickening of the years.

Last year, in June, I awoke very early one morning. I sleep less and less these days and most mornings I'm alert by seven o'clock. But that day I was up and padding about before five. About six-thirty I walked up the village looking for something to do. We've a new recreation ground and I turned in there. The place has grown a lot during the last few years, new houses, new young people, and somehow it was decided that we ought to have a recreation field; tennis courts, football fields, swings and roundabouts for the little ones, the lot. I'm on the committee for the provision of this field and I thought I might look at what progress was being made.

The place lies behind houses and there's a drive of about a hundred and fifty yards to reach it. The work had been nicely done and I walked along, admiring the rolled surface, the neat fencing. A little car park stands at the end of the drive, next to the hard courts, and a car was already there. I assumed that it belonged to someone living nearby, that it had been left there overnight. I began to walk along the field's boundary, near the hedge. The light dew was almost off the grass and cuttings from the mower were dry and flaky on the surface, although you could still see where a bird had disturbed the direction of the grass earlier. I hadn't gone far when I heard a shout. Someone climbed out of the parked car and waved to me. It was Charlie Betson. He came up to me, grinning.

At first I thought there was something wrong with him, but he was all right. He was very thin and he walked loosely, arms dangling and feet planting themselves aimlessly at the end of irregular strides. He held his head far back, as if to compensate for the loss of his old, controlled, straight-backed dignity. This worried me for a while, but he spoke well and naturally, telling me of his job. He was felling a stand of beech on an estate some miles away; I knew the trees well. We walked along the mixed hedge at the end of the field, blackthorn mainly, with a bit of scrub oak and some maple, and we heard something rustling on the other side.

"Heron," said Charlie. "That's a heron in the wet ditch. There's always one there, between the old gravel pond and the mill. Good picking in the ditch for herons, plenty of frogs and that."

He smiled.

"My old dad," he said, "told me about him when I was small. Finest poacher in the country was my dad, and he told me about the heron. There was one in the ditch when he was a boy, and I reckon there always will be one. After my day, I expect."

We poked a branch through the hedge and the long heron rose slowly, his legs trailing, and flew towards the mill. We watched him go.

"What was between your father," I asked carefully, "and Bill Francis?"

"Well," said Charlie, "much of an age, weren't they? Went to school together, grew up together, young men together. Bill Francis could beat my dad all along the line. He was stronger, he could fight better, people liked him more. And even with a gun, why, Bill could always beat my dad. Best shot I ever see was Bill Francis. My dad always gave him credit. Rivals, they were."

He cocked an amused eye down at me.

"Of course," he said, "in the end my father won."

"How's that?" I said.

"We've always been here," said Charlie, "Betson and Francis. Those are the true names in this village. My father had nine boys, counting Archie who got killed in the war; Bill Francis never had any. There ain't no Francis left."

We walked quietly back down the field.

"Old Bill liked you, didn't he?" asked Charlie.

"He did," I said. "He wanted to leave me his fields."

"Yeah, well." Charlie picked up a stone and flung it away. "Understandable, that is. You should have let him. You're about the same age as my oldest brother."

We reached his car and I looked inside. It was perfectly neat and clean, Charlie's racing paper open on the seat the one untidy object.

"It's the wife," said Charlie. "She cleans everything, car, house, kids, me . . . there's no rest."

"Charlie," I said, "why are you down here so early? It's not seven o'clock."

He lowered his head, suddenly heavy and obstinate. The skin of his face was thickening and coarsening as his father's had, and deep folds were appearing at the sides of his nose and under his cheekbones. When he looked up, I saw that his teeth were lined and spotted.

He got into the car and picked up his paper, folding it uneasily. I could see in him so clearly the graceless, shy boy he had been.

"It's quieter," he said. "It's much quieter. I get up most mornings and go on down to my mother's for breakfast. Then I bring the paper up here and pick a few winners."

He sat there uncomfortably, as if he didn't care, his face sad and heavy, looking at something far away.

"You don't know what it's like," he said, "living somewhere else. Do you know who lives next door to me? Gypsies, that's who. And it's the same everywhere, all strangers. Down here, it's quieter and I know everybody. My family, and that. It's nicer."

I didn't say anything.

"It's lovely here," said Charlie, "in the morning, in the early morning."

"What are your runners today?" I said loudly. "What do you fancy?"

He began to read some names out of his paper.

"Is there a gray in the big race?" I said.

I was wasting time. I would have been glad to leave; I wanted some neat conclusion to our meeting.

"You like grays?" Charlie asked.

"Yes," I said. "A couple of years ago I went to a breeding stables in Yorkshire where they had a gray stallion. Abernant was his name—he had a lot of gray offspring, you couldn't miss them. Beautiful size, wonderful clean, round bone, and such neat, intelligent heads. Good stuff, they were."

Charlie laughed. The life was back in his eyes.

"You don't want to bother about color," he said. "A good horse is never a bad color. I'll be better off picking my own winners."

I went away down the road. The morning was beautiful, the afternoon cloudless and very hot. About eight that evening, as a small, cool wind began, Charlie came into the garden. He was waving a thin bundle of notes.

"Here you are," he called. "Two pounds at eight to one, that's sixteen pounds!"

He was delighted with himself.

"What's all this?" I said.

I was astonished at the change in Charlie. He was inches taller than he had been that morning, he moved with all his remembered certainty and assurance.

"I put two pounds on the gray for you," he said, "and five for myself. We've had a good day."

"What gray?" I said, bewildered.

"Ah, you're a sly one," he said. "You're as cunning as a cartload. You knew all the time a gray by Abernant was going in that race. Well, you've done us both a bit of good."

He pushed the notes at me.

"I can't take these, Charlie," I said. "Give them to the children."

"They're yours," he said, roughly. "The kids get plenty. Take the money—if the horse had lost I'd have been around here for the two pounds' stake, don't worry."

"If you're sure," I said.

I took the money from him and at once he moved away, waving as he went. He was full of bounce. I wondered how, that morning, I had thought him changed in any way, how anything could have so filled me with false foreboding.

That was the last time I spoke to Charlie.

Last week I heard that Charlie was missing, hadn't been seen for two days. I can't remember how I learned this; by the sort of osmosis that happens in a village, I expect. I was neither surprised nor had I expected this news. I was just filled with an unthinking certainty. As soon as I heard I took the car out and went to the recreation field. I drove through the car park and across the field itself, right to the far end. When I got out I was moving very stiffly, as if my body were a new and intricate mechanism come newly to me. I remember my eyes so tight and stiff that it would have been impossible to blink without singleminded and deliberate effort. I broke through the hedge and the heron got up about fifty yards away. A single flap of his wings turned him into the wind and he vanished over the elms.

Charlie was there, almost at my feet. He was lying there quite peacefully, untouched almost, if you didn't look too closely. His gun was at his side, the muzzle under his chest. I slid it out and walked down the ditch. One barrel was still loaded. A pigeon flew up from the noise of my walking and I shot it casually, brought it back, and put it obviously in the field about ten yards from Charlie. Then I placed the gun near his fallen hand. We're a close lot in this village, look after our own. Almost the first thing old Bill Francis said to me, that was.

When I got home, I thought about it, hard. I wasn't shocked, or stunned; I was just completely sad. I'd recognized something in Charlie that last day, without knowing it, some intuition had prepared me. I got it all clear in my mind and walked over to the police house. Sergeant Watson is a sensible man, made no fuss, and the official business began.

Yesterday I went to the funeral, simple enough. Charlie's mother asked me. She came up to the house early this week, sat on the edge of a chair, and said that she expected to see me there. The church was full of young men, Charlie's friends, and in front sat a row of Betsons, tall and hard-faced. Afterwards Charlie's wife asked me back to his mother's house to have a meal. I thought of refusing, but at her side was Charlie's oldest sister, fair-haired and implacable. The enormous Betson men were already there when I arrived, talking in their quiet, heavy voices. One by one they came up to me, shook my hand, told me that Charlie had spoken of me often, always boasted of how I had taught him to read.

"He liked you," they said. "Charlie liked you. He always gave you credit."

I sat there, my plate on my knee, drinking the strong, hot tea. After a while Charlie's mother came over. She was a very old lady and she sat silent and upright opposite me. I tried to tell her that it had been a good occasion, that Charlie would have been glad to know that so many of his friends had come to wish him good-bye. Her face was calm and without expression, but there was that in her eyes which would not be comforted.

"He was a good boy," she said, "but he was lost. He needed safety. All my boys need safety, like their father before them. People think when they see my lovely boys, strong and proud, that nothing could ever worry them. But it's not true."

One of the daughters stood by the table, warily, listening carefully.

"When Archie went to the war," said Mrs. Betson, "when he was eighteen, the oldest of them, I watched him going nearly mad away from us. My boys need to be in the fields about us, nearby, where their father walked before them, where they feel safe. They need a house where their brothers are only a shout away and there's food and drink without fuss, any time of the day or night."

The room was very still. Charlie's brothers, listening uncomfortably to their mother's unlikely eloquence, stared blankly about.

"I knew he was going lost," said Mrs. Betson. "I knew Charlie was going lost when he started coming over here every morning, six o'clock, five o'clock. He never went to Brighton, did you know that? In all his life Charlie never went as far away as Brighton."

The sisters began to move about, making things orderly. They gave tea and food to brothers and nephews, they arranged them in little groups, they sent them into the garden to walk between the rows of beans and potatoes. The world began to look safe and normal.

"We won't forget what you've done," said Mrs. Betson. "We've guessed what you've done, and we shan't forget it."

I stood up and said good-bye. The whole house was suddenly more cheerful and brisk, the day brighter. One or two of the men lifted a hand to me as I left, but most of them smoked and talked together, ignoring me.

And all day I've sat here in the garden thinking of the handsome Betson men, golden as Vikings, walking safe in the little world of our one street and its handful of fields. I thought of Charlie, who might be dead because he had left that simple and limited world for one where he had been forced to make decisions and live in a frightening freedom. But most of all I've been thinking of old Bill Francis, who had spent his life watching over the village and who hadn't any sons at all.

꩜ Snowdrops

Today Miss Webster was going to show them the snowdrops growing in the little three-cornered garden outside the school-keeper's house, where they weren't allowed to go. All through the winter, Miss Webster said, the snowdrops had been asleep under the ground, but now they were up, growing in the garden. He tried to think what they would look like, but all he could imagine was one flake of the falling snow, bitterly frail and white, and nothing like a flower.

It was a very cold morning. He leaned against the kitchen table, feeling the hard edge against his chest, eating his breakfast slowly. His brother, Geraint, who was only three, sat in an armchair close to the fire. He could see the shape of Geraint's head outlined against the flames and he saw with wonder that the fire had given to his brother's legs a glow of red only slightly less bright than the leaping flames. Geraint was eating a bowl of porridge, and what he did was this. He would make a crater in the porridge with his spoon, and then he'd watch the milk run in and fill the hole up. Then he would dip his spoon in the milk and drink it. The boy watched his brother.

"Hurry up," said the boy's mother, "or you'll never get to school!"

"Miss Webster is going to show us the snowdrops today," he said.

"That's nice," said his mother, looking out of the window at the gray morning. "I wonder where your father is."

His father came in and filled the room with bigness. He stood in front of the fire, because it was cold in the yard, and all the boy could see was a faint light each side of his father's wide body.

"It's a cold wind," said his father. "I can't remember a colder March."

The man turned around and faced them, smiling because he was much warmer and the cold March wind was safely locked outside the house.

"You're a big boy for six," he said to the boy, "and it's all because you eat your breakfast up."

This was a joke his father always said, and the boy smiled, thinking all the time of the snowdrops. Would it be too cold to go and see them? Perhaps Miss Webster would take only the boys, he comforted himself, because they were stronger, and the girls could stay in school out of the cold.

"The Meredith boy is being buried this afternoon," his father was saying to his mother. "I'm sorry I shan't be able to go. I worked with his father for two and a half years, up at the rolling mill. A nice man, Charlie Meredith, very quiet. I hear he's very cut up, and his wife too. This was their only boy."

"How old was he?" asked his mother.

"Twenty," his father said. "Twenty last January. Silly little fool. That bike was too powerful for him—well, to go at that speed on a wet, dark night. Over seventy, the police said, straight into the back of a stationary truck. A terrible mess."

"He was a nice-looking boy, too," said his mother.

"All the Merediths are," said his father. "This one was very friendly with the young teacher up at the school, Webber, is it? Something like that."

But his mother coughed and looked sharply at the boy.

"Oh?" said his father. "Of course. I should have remembered. Come on, son, or you'll be late."

It seemed much warmer when he got to school and he

took off his overcoat next to Edmund Jenkins. Edmund had a long blue scarf which his big sister had knitted for him. They each held an end of the scarf and raced up the corridor, seeing how many children they could catch, but Miss Lewis stopped them. Then Edmund told him a joke.

"What's the biggest rope in the world?" Edmund asked.

The boy didn't know.

"Europe," said Edmund, and they both laughed.

They were still laughing as they went into the classroom, although Miss Webster wasn't there. After a time Miss Lewis came in and sent the children into other classrooms. Miss Lewis took the top class and she was very stern and strict. He and Edmund had to go to Miss Lewis' class.

"Europe," said Edmund Jenkins to him, very quietly, as they went into the top class. Edmund was very brave.

It wasn't too bad in Miss Lewis' class, because they had some interesting books there and the arithmetic was not difficult. When you looked out of the window, too, you saw a different part of the playground. The boy could almost see a corner of the school-keeper's house, so he wasn't very far away from the snowdrops.

Just before playtime Miss Lewis told all the children from Miss Webster's class that they could go back to their own room after play. The boy grinned in delight. Everything would be all right, he told himself. After play they would surely go to see the flowers.

Out in the playground they all began to run about, except Gerald Davis, who seemed to fall over whatever he did. He was quite unable to make even the tiniest step without tumbling down, and his face was red from laughing and because he didn't know what was happening to him. Edmund Jenkins was standing close by and the boy could see that Edmund had been up to his tricks again.

"What's happening to Gerald?" he asked.

But Edmund only pointed to Gerald's boots, and then the boy saw that his laces had been tied together, the left boot to the right boot and the right boot to the left boot, so that

Gerald was hobbled. Some boys were beginning to imitate Gerald, falling about although their boots weren't tied together. After a while he and Edmund untied the laces and Gerald went whooping up the gravel yard like a released pigeon.

He walked with Edmund towards the last corner of the playground, away from the wind, and they took their small packets of sandwiches from their pockets. Edmund had three sandwiches, with marmalade in them, and he had two sandwiches, but he didn't know what they were filled with. He bit one of them to find out.

The taste was incredibly new and marvellous, filling the whole of his mouth with delight and pleasure. He shook his head to show Edmund how wonderful the taste was, and then let Edmund have a bite.

"What's in it, Edmund?" he asked. "What's in my sandwich?"

"Bacon," said Edmund. "It's only bacon."

The boy was incredulous. He opened the second sandwich to inspect the filling. It didn't look like bacon.

"It can't be," he said. "I have bacon for my breakfast every morning. I had some *this* morning."

"I know," said Edmund, "but it tastes different when it's cold."

Together they walked as far as the shed in which the coal was stored. This was as far as they were allowed to go. Not very far away, but tantalizingly around the corner and down the little path that led to the garden, the snowdrops were growing.

"Do you wish," said the boy, "that Miss Webster will take us to see the flowers when play is over?"

"I don't care," said Edmund, "because I've seen some already, growing in my aunt's garden."

The boy looked at his best friend, deciding carefully whether he would ask him to describe a snowdrop. But he would wait, he thought, to see them for himself, and then the bell was ringing to call them in.

The children cheered and clapped when they saw Miss Webster. She was dressed in a black frock, without any jewelry, but she smiled at them, holding her finger to her lips for them to be quiet. The bandage she had on one finger, where she had trapped it in the cupboard door and hadn't cried, looked very white and clean. She gave them some crayons and a big sheet of paper for each child and they could draw whatever they liked.

The boy drew a robin. He hadn't drawn a robin since Christmas, but just recently he had been watching one that came to his garden every day, and now he knew just how the bird's head fitted onto his round little body, and he had seen the way the legs, as thin as pieces of wire, splayed out underneath. Sometimes the robin looked like a hunchback, but he would draw this robin standing up bravely, throwing out his red chest before he sang. And the robin's song was odd. It wasn't very long, and it dropped and fell like threads of falling water. The boy closed his eyes a little while so that he could hear the robin, but he couldn't get it quite right. Soon he was engrossed in watching his robin grow on the paper. With infinite care he set its delicate feet on a brown twig, not just a flat stick as he had drawn at Christmas, but a real twig, with little knobs on it where the buds would be. At last it was finished and he leaned back in his chair, looking around as he did so. Nearly all the other children had completed their drawings some time before and they were reading their books. Miss Webster was sitting at her desk, her head in her hands. Everything was very still. The boy took out his book and began to read, but most of the time he looked at the robin he had drawn.

This is what he was doing when the bell ended morning school and they were dismissed for home. Miss Webster looked at his robin and she liked it. She took it from his desk and pinned it in a good place on the wall, where everybody could see it. The boy was pleased and surprised, because he had never before had a drawing pinned up in this way, although he knew he could draw at least as well as

Edmund, who had a drawing selected nearly every week.

"Shall we be going to see the snowdrops this afternoon?" he asked Miss Webster before he went home.

"Yes," she said, "if Miss Lewis will allow us, we'll go to see them this afternoon."

He ate his lunch quietly, thinking in his head of a story about a wizard who could change himself into anything at all. It was a good story, but something always seemed to happen before he got to the end of it. Sometimes he began it at night in bed, only to fall asleep long before the really exciting part. Now his mother was talking to him.

"Was Miss Webster in school this morning?" she asked.

His mother was knitting a pullover. The needles went over and under each other, with the same little slide and click, and a row of knitting grew magically behind them.

"Yes," he said, "but she came late. She didn't arrive until playtime."

"Poor girl," said his mother.

He thought about this for a long time.

"She's got a bad hand," he said. "She caught her finger in the cupboard door and her hand was bleeding. She's got a bandage on it today. She'll never be able to bend her finger again, that's what Edmund Jenkins said."

"Oh, you and Edmund Jenkins," said his mother.

He raced back to school, his boots ringing on the pavement as they always seemed to in cold weather. Every day he went a special way, over the river bridge, being very careful of the traffic, up Penry Street as far as the fruiterer's, then across the road by the fire station in case the doors were open; now he could balance along a low wall outside Jack Williams' garden, and at last he was in the small road where the school was. He never knew what would happen here, because he would meet many boys going to school and almost any adventure could happen. Once in this road Bernard Spencer had given him a glass marble, and once he and Edmund had found a silver medal which somebody had won for running. Edmund's father had taken it to the police, but they didn't have a reward.

But there was nobody about, except some girls skipping and giggling just inside the school yard, and he made his way inside the building. Everybody was sitting very quietly inside the classroom. They were allowed to go in early because it was very cold. Normally they would have stayed outside until Miss Lewis rang the bell, and some boys stayed outside however wet and cold it was, but today it seemed that they all wanted to sit quietly with Miss Webster, close to the cast-iron stove that had the figure of a tortoise on the top.

At two o'clock Miss Webster marked her register and then began to tell them a story. It was a good story, about a dragon who guarded a hoard of treasure in his den underground, where the snowdrops slept all through the winter. From time to time Miss Webster turned her head to look at the big clock in the hall. She could see it through the top half of the classroom door, which had four panes of glass in it. Her voice seemed to be hoarser than usual, which was fine when she read the dragon's bits, but not good for the knight nor the princess. She shut her book with a snap and stood up. She hadn't completed the story.

"Now we'll go to see the snowdrops," she said. "I want the girls to go quietly to the cloakroom and put on their coats. When they are ready, I'll come along with the boys. Everybody must wear a coat. If you have difficulty with buttons, please stand in front and I'll fasten them for you."

He stood up with a sudden lightening of the heart. He had known all the time that Miss Webster would not forget, and at last she was taking him to see the miraculous flowers, pale and fragile as the falling snow. He looked at Miss Webster with gratitude. Her eyes were bright as frost, and she was making sure that the girls walked nicely through the door. Edmund Jenkins waved at him and that was funny, because Edmund had his black gloves on, with a hole in a place he could push his finger through. Edmund waved his finger like a fat white worm in the middle of his dark hand.

They all walked beautifully through the playground, in two rows holding hands, and he held Edmund's hand and they gave a little skip together every three steps. It didn't take long to get to the garden. The children bent down, four at a time, to look at the little clump of snowdrops and Miss Webster told them what to look at. He and Edmund would be the last to look. When they had finished, the other children went down to the garden gate which opened onto the road. It was a big gate with iron bars and your head could almost poke through. Somewhere a long way off the boy could hear men singing. They sang softly, mournfully, the words carried gently on the air over the school wall, but the boy could not hear what they said.

"It's a funeral," said Edmund. "My father's there and my Uncle Jim. It's a boy who was killed on a motor-bike."

The boy nodded. Funerals often passed the school on their way to the cemetery at the top of the valley. All the men wore black suits and they walked slowly. Sometimes they sang.

He squatted down to look at the snowdrops. He felt a slow, sad disappointment. He looked around for Miss Webster to explain these simple flowers to him, but she had gone down to the gate and was staring through, looking up the road. Her back was as hard as a stone. He turned again to the snowdrops, concentrating, willing them to turn marvellous in front of his eyes. They hung down their four-petalled heads in front of him, the white tinged with minute green, the little green ball sturdily holding the petals, the grayish leaves standing up like miniature spears. The boy began to see their fragility. He saw them blow in a sudden gust of the cold March wind, shake, and straighten gallantly. He imagined them standing all night in the dark garden, holding bravely to their specks of whiteness. He put out a finger to touch the nearest flower, knowing now what snowdrops were. He lifted his face to tell Miss Webster, but she was standing right at the gate, holding the iron bars with her hands. Her shoulders were shaking.

> *Mor ddedwydd yw y rhai trwy ffydd*
> *S'yn mynd o blith y byw . . .*

sang the men as they filed solemnly past the school. The boy knew it was Welsh because of his grandmother, and it was sad and beautiful.

After a while they couldn't hear the singing any more, but Miss Webster continued to cry aloud in the midst of the frightened children.

Prey

When the cold weather came, the sky was suddenly full of hawks. Not great flocks of them, as with communal birds, but hawks were suddenly more plentiful; wherever I went, when I looked up, somewhere, at the corner of eyesight, there would be a still point in the moving sky. A hawk, a kestrel, hovering.

In the spring a motorway was completed north of the village, two straight wide roads cut parallel through the brown dirt. For months huge earth-shifters and diggers churned through the land, but in spring all was done. The soft banks of little severed hills made easy burrowing, and in moved colonies of rats and voles and rabbits. Hawks hang on a rope of high air above the scurrying traffic, stationed at intervals along the road. I understand this. I know just where the favored vantage points are on that highway. Often the birds, still as porcelain, keep unceasing watch above a crossroads or an intersection, or hammer into the grass for a prey invisible to me as I drive past. They claim, too, the small bodies of creatures freshly killed on the roads. I know why the hawks watch there.

But with the frost, the hawks, the autumn-colored birds, seemed to be more numerous. I saw a kestrel high over Ernie Foster's big field where I'd never seen one before, not in twenty years. I saw it there, intent, hanging, a machine for looking and killing. I put the glasses on him so that I could watch him make his sudden little shifts as he changed his wing-tip hold on the wind, the swift flutter of tail and finger-ends as he adjusted his view of the upturned world. That morning I counted ten of them, hawks, high and solitary, as I drove the dozen miles to town. Then, in the evening, one was mercilessly beating the hedge at the side of the house.

Years ago, one swooped almost into my windscreen as I drove under the downs. He came late out of his dive, wings and legs braced in front of the glass. I saw the open hook of his beak, his furious yellow eye.

Now that winter is complete and the sky uninterrupted between the stripped bones of trees, I can see the sentinel hawks.

All my life I have been on the side of the small birds against the hawks. Two weeks ago I went down to the beach in the teeth of the wind. I left the car at the top of the sea lane and walked down past the six old cottages. They were shut fast, huddled shut as the blunt wind bundled round them. It was bitterly cold on the unsheltered beach and my eyes wept. I wrapped my coat more tightly about me, knowing the gesture useless, as I walked the path above the sand. Spray and fragmentary sand spat and stung in the working storm. On the rim of the beach grows a straggle of blackthorns, bent almost to the ground after constant struggle with salty gales. Their bare stems shone red and mulberry in the sun. Above them stood a hawk, a yard or two above them, balancing in the wild gusts. As I looked, he cut through the wind like a winged blade, sweeping along the thicket, raking it, driving the little birds out before him. He failed to make his kill.

Then the desperate small finches burst out in a cloud at him, into his jaws and talons, with such pugnacity, such unanimous bravery, that the big hawk sheered off, discomfited. I could have cheered those charging ounces; but at once the hawk resumed his iron station, holding himself a yard above the bushes, hanging and ready. I began to run toward him. Stumbling and clumsy in gumboots I ran, clapping my hands, shouting into the wind. But the scared birds flew out in puffs in front of me, like sparks struck from the iron they dived into the light, and the killing hawk was among them. In my fury I had done the hawk's work. He turned with magnificent leisure above the plowland and flopped heavily out of sight. I should have pitied those torn birds, but I was elated, elated. I left the harried flock in turmoil behind me, under their flimsy twigs.

Goshawk, sparrow hawk, buzzard, kite, harrier, falcon, arrogant killing birds. And peregrine and merlin.

It was the last Monday in October, after the first frosts and when I was newly aware of the watching hawks of the cold weather, that I went to London. My appointment was at noon, so I went by train at mid-morning. I stood on the platform, and the weather was the clear calm often normal for that time of the year, still and clear, not so much cold as lacking in heat, like early morning in Spain. All the color was golden, the deep gold of the turned furrows, yellow gold of the stubble, the sun turning pale gold the white of road and stone. One hawk, a kestrel, burned in the sky.

But all along the journey the birds held their watching posts on clifftops of air. High above the Arun River, they held the water meadows in the wholeness of their gaze, over widening Surrey they positioned themselves at their perfect heights or beat the thinning woods for rodent or frail bird. At the end of their eyes' range they handed over to other hanging hawks. The train was not for a moment unobserved, nor was any corner of a field, nor twitch of grass, nor lift of smoke. In London itself, only those under the safety of roofs went privately about their business. Kestrels and sparrow hawks hovered over the great parks at the heart of London. England lay under the hawk's eye.

And hawks invisible to us circle tightly the high supporting air, set high in their appointed places. At first light I walk into my garden and I am aware of them. I find on my lawn each day the evidence of hawks; a ring of thrush's feathers, skin still on the quills, where the kill has been fastidiously plucked, and sometimes a delicate claw. When I walk in the beech woods I see beheaded shrews limp-tailed in the grass.

How they bleat in harmless flocks, the weak birds. Dove, thrush, bunting, plover, warbler, pipit, those vulnerable names.

On Sunday Dennis came to see me. He comes seldom to my house, for he is a busy man, active in public causes, forever attending committees and meetings. He talks incessantly, the soft words grow about him. I cannot imagine that he is ever alone. He was in bountiful form, expansive, telling me of a jungle of small injustices, urging me to support this or that community action.

"All together," he said. "That's the answer. We should all pull together."

I rarely answer Dennis. For all his kindness and endless patience, I am indifferent to him. Leaning back in my chair, away from his optimistic voice, I saw the kestrel, a female, hovering outside my window. She was so near I felt I could almost touch her. I saw the clear outline of her every feather. Rust brown, bracken brown, red where the light got to her, her back and her long slim tail were barred with strips of darker color. Her head turned down and her yellow eye blazed with her one purpose. I stood at the center of the room and watched her, watched her, while Dennis, on his feet at the window, waved and squeaked. He put his glasses over his feeble eyes and chattered. The sight of the hawk there, within feet of him, was for him a miracle; but I stood still, seeing her scaled legs and her unblinking eye, and said nothing. When she released herself into her swoop she moved more slowly than I had expected, and on the ground, in the coarse grass at the garden's edge, she was ungainly and fumbling. But she arose powerfully, holding in her talons a plump rat, dead in the closed grip. I told Dennis I had work to do, and he left. After that intent and ominous bird, his gossiping voice annoyed me.

In Spain I saw the great eagles; the golden eagle, the imperial eagle, once only the tawny eagle, strayed by chance from middle Europe. How they flew, the great birds, majestically gliding and soaring, an occasional flap of great vanes holding them far above the tiny world. They held aloft their arrogant, drifting flight, crucified against the moving sky.

But I liked best the smaller birds, Bonelli's eagle and particularly the common booted eagle, smaller than a buzzard. I would watch them, never far from trees, wheel and cry in the hot morning air, those graceful birds. I saw them often when they perched on high posts or in the branches of single trees. I would stand nearby or walk beneath them, looking up at their mottled bodies. They did not see me, I was not an essential part of the world in which they lived. Hunched and contemptuous, they ignored me. But when they saw what they wanted, a small bird or animal, they became sleek and intent and I knew their yellow eyes had sharpened and focused on that one life, that the yellow concentration of their eyes was turned like a searchlight and that all outside it was dark to the hunting bird. The birds of prey have created a simple world for themselves, sifting and rejecting through their superbly organized senses all that is not necessary. All morning I would watch them, the booted eagles, until with a lift or two of the wings they took themselves into a rising current.

I've twice dreamed about hawks, vividly, memorably. In the first dream I saw a hawk on the ground, on a rock, standing among foliage of brilliant emerald color. He was quite magnificent. All about him, on the ground and in the air, were the soft birds and animals on which he preyed, wood pigeons, mice, fat moles, voles, rats. Yet he cried petulantly, his voice harsh and wailing, and when he moved I saw that he was a crippled hawk, that one leg stuck out awkwardly from him, thin and withered, the vise of his crushing foot impotent. The second dream was darker and less detailed, and all I remember clearly is the image of a hooded falcon on an ebony perch. He was quite still. His jesses were loose about his legs, and I could see them in the light of a candle or an oil lamp which stood nearby. But his hood was extraordinary. It was stitched and embossed with so meticulous an artistry that it seemed, extravagant though it was, almost a part of the natural bird. Its polished leather, stained purple and scarlet, held all the light. Blunt and eyeless, the decorated head on the unmoving bird gave to the falcon a heraldic power. I pitied both those birds and think often of them.

All week I have been muttering to myself Yeats' line, "Being high and solitary and most stern," which is not about a hawk at all. The hawk is his own man, makes his own decisions, which are of death. He does not kill wantonly, but to fulfill his simple, orderly purpose. There is no chaos in his world, nor reason. He will kill or die.

As I drove home this evening I did not see the kestrel over Ernie Foster's big field, although I stopped the car and waited for ten minutes. It was very cold and a thick frost already furred the bars of the field gate, and the ground was iron. But you can't deny a hawk's nature. He'll be there tomorrow, spread wing, eye, hook, and ripping claw.

A Moonlight Gallop

Most weekends when the weather was good enough I used to go cycling in the mountains, usually the Brecon Beacons or the Black Mountains near the Herefordshire border. At that time, when I was about fifteen, I used to belong to the Youth Hostel Association, and so did Del Wellington and Charlie Bond, my friends. We used to pay a membership fee of five shillings a year and in return we got an enamel badge and a card to show we belonged to the Association; we were also sent a map which showed the location of all the Youth Hostels, most of them remote farmhouses, where we could stay for a night or two. Occasionally during the winter we'd plan, with the help of such a map, an immense journey through the dales of Yorkshire, unimaginably distant and foreign, knowing we'd never get there.

We knew all the hostels within possible cycling distance of our homes, although we rarely used them. Del's father had given us a heavy tent, already old, and we preferred to lug this about with us. We must have looked very odd on our three decrepit cycles—mine was rescued from the scrapyard and restored with loving care and some curious homemade fittings—all our strange equipment tied about us. Del always carried the tent on his bike, its bulk of canvas folded in an awkward sausage and slung beneath his cross-bar. It was so big that he had to ride bowlegged.

We had great times. Once we camped on a high moor in mid-Wales and I awoke in the middle of the night. I poked

104

my head out of the tent into a moonlight whiter than frost, and all around us, still as wool, the sheep stood, hundreds of them, staring at the tent. I got back into my blankets and went to sleep and when the morning came there were no sheep to be seen anywhere. I didn't say a word about them to Del and Charlie.

I remember, too, camping near the foot of a waterfall. We hadn't meant to stay overnight, but we'd been attracted by the voice of the water, had pushed our bikes over a wet meadow towards the stream, and followed it up about four hundred yards until we reached the waterfall. It wasn't very high, perhaps sixty feet, but it was perfect. The white fall, never more than a foot wide, bent slowly over a ledge of rock and dropped without check into the pool beneath. We bathed in this pool. It was deep, cold enough to make us gasp, and the cleanest water I have ever used. It made our skins unrecognizable to us, as if a slippery layer of something had been stripped off us for the first time in our lives.

It took us quite a while to drag our gear up to the pool, and it wasn't easy to pitch our tent there, but we did it at last and went to sleep listening to the water's muted thunder. In the morning the green sun filtered down to us through the overhanging branches of the trees overhead, and through the nodding ferns on the wet rocks. I could have stayed there forever.

That year we got away as often as we could. Perhaps it was a natural restlessness, the wish to see over the next hill, and the next; perhaps we realized that time was already beginning to run out for us, that there were responsibilities we would have to recognize, as well as the attractions of more sophisticated and less perfect pleasures. Whatever it was, hardly a week went by without us moving north into the deep mountains, slowly through the little villages climbing the one road out, merrily over the bare uplands guarded by buzzards. After a while we ventured farther afield; leaving our tent behind and using the Youth Hostels.

Towards the end of July the weather turned unseasonably

bad. There was heavy rain, and a brutal wind sprang up in the evenings. The last Friday was depressing and we decided at school that we could go nowhere that weekend. I got home about five and began to read, eating some food aimlessly and without savor. The doorbell rang and my mother answered it. After a little while Charlie Bond came in. He had his cycle cape over his shoulders. It was black, with a hood.

"What do you think?" said Charlie.

I looked out of the window. The rain had stopped and a faint, watery sun showed tentatively behind the clouds.

"I don't know," I said.

"It'll be good," said Charlie. "The wind's dropped and it's cool enough for a fast ride. Del's coming."

"Mrs. Wellington is never going to let Del go out in this weather!" said my mother. "There must be something wrong with her! Well, you're not going, my boy, so don't ask it."

The way she spoke I knew it was all right, so I grinned at her and got ready. I pushed my bike outside—Charlie's was leaning against the kerb.

"Where's Del?" I said.

"I haven't been over yet," said Charlie. "I only said he was coming so that it would be easier to persuade your mother."

Together we called for Del and I suppose we were on our way before six o'clock. Everything went right for us. Before we were out of town the sun was shining and the evening had miraculously cleared. Without our tent we went at a fast clip, and there seemed about us all a surplus of energy which we controlled and directed into the expert handling of our cycles. We were over the crest of the mountain and dropping down into Abergavenny by seven. I can't remember that we ever had a better ride, the roads clear and kind, and we knowing each other so well that there was no need for talking.

Del had the maps, and he led us out on the Hereford road for a few miles before turning left onto a narrow lane. The light was still good and the sky unclouded above the valley along which we rode. I've never been in so still a place. Although we passed a few cottages at the side of the road, we saw nobody. It was as if the whole valley were deserted, its windows blind to our passing.

We began to climb, very gently at first, and the hollow valley opened out a little. The hedges were smaller and scrubbier and we could see over them into the fields they protected. As we climbed we could see, a long way off, the ruins of an abbey, its solid wall so pierced by the procession of great arched windows through which we saw the lit hills behind that it appeared insubstantial, a tracery of stone. The long evening sun shone fully upon it, on the tall decay of its towers, on its useless pillars. When at last we reached it, we found it standing back off the road, about two hundred yards back. We went in and wandered about for a bit, leaving our bikes leaning against the hedge. Charlie Bond, his hands hidden in his cycle cape, the black hood on his head, stepped mournfully through the cloisters, intoning as he went. He was a brilliant mimic, was Charlie. He could sing so exactly like Bing Crosby that Eustace Berry, a boy in our class, used to come miles out of his way just to walk to school with Charlie, listening to him sing. Now Charlie trod softly on the grass between the fallen walls, his face hidden under his cowl, his echoing, faulty Latin moving and ominous. It was amusing too, but I was glad when Del said, "Stow it, Charlie. We've still got a fair way to go."

And at once I became aware of the fading light. Back down the valley there was a hint of twilight about the farms and the tall trees, and a soft mist was beginning to fill the fields near the river.

"That's for heat," said Charlie. "Positively it will be very hot tomorrow."

"I worry about tonight," Del said. "We have to be in the hostel by nine, and then we have our supper to cook. I'm starving."

We had a look at the large-scale map. We had at least five miles to go and up hills so steep that the contour lines pressed hard against each other.

"Look at those lines," said Charlie. "They'd depress an active goat."

We swung our legs over our saddles and rode on. Pretty soon, so steep had the climb become, we were forced to dismount and push the bikes. The fields had given way to harsh moorland, cropped by ponies. Here and there the heather and poor grass were broken by stony outcrops. Nothing moved at all. The long shadows merged imperceptibly into a continuous darkness.

"We'll be late," Del said.

"If we find it," said Charlie.

Del only grunted. This was a hostel we had never visited, but we had seen it often enough on the map. We knew exactly where it was. We pushed on, searching the moor for a light. The moon came up, brilliantly lucid, and we felt more cheerful, singing gently together.

It was Del who saw the light, high on our left hand, and he led us without a falter along the rough path which led to the house. We were all glad to get there and laughed and joked as we knocked on the door. It was nearly ten o'clock.

Mrs. Devereux let us in. She was the warden's wife, a tall, unfriendly woman. When she spoke, her voice was slow and surprisingly soft and she spoke with a Midlands accent. I thought she might have come from Birmingham. Her husband stood silently in the kitchen. They were not welcoming.

"You boys are late," he said.

"I know," I answered. "We're sorry. We didn't know the climb would be so steep—we thought we had plenty of time."

"You know the rules," he said. "I'd be within my rights to turn you away."

We stood there, not answering.

"They might as well stay, Jack," said Mrs. Devereux, timidly. "There's nobody else here. They look tired."

He didn't answer so I took his silence for agreement.

"We'll bring the bikes in," I said.

He looked at me for the first time, leaning, his hands flat on the kitchen table. He was a stocky man, his broad shoulders filling the flannel shirt he wore, but his face was worn tight down almost to the bone and his eyes were set deep. There was no expression at all on his face, unless it was a kind of impersonal weariness.

We went outside to bring in the cycles.

"Leave them in the passage," said Mr. Devereux as we went.

Outside, in the light of the one electric bulb set high in the wall, I looked at Del and Charlie. They looked quiet and withdrawn, and they did not meet my gaze.

"Cheer up, boys," I said.

"You must be mad," said Del, "but speak to me after supper."

When we got back in I asked Mr. Devereux where we could cook our supper.

"There'll be no cooking here," he said.

"But we've had nothing to eat for hours," I protested, indignation making my voice sharp. "You can let us heat a can of beans, at least!"

Del and Charlie stood behind me, saying nothing, leaving it to me. Mr. Devereux looked from one to the other of us, his dead face empty. He waved a hand briefly.

"The wife will give you a mug of cocoa," he said, "and if you have bread and cheese you can eat that."

We settled for that, sitting around the scrubbed table. The cocoa was scaldingly hot and sweet and we drank it without a word. Devereux and his wife sat each side of the fireplace, on long settles. There was an unbelievably tense air about them and they never stopped watching us. The second that Charlie finished his food, Devereux stood up.

"Come on," he said, "I'll show you the dormitory."

We collected our sleeping bags and our rucksacks and followed him out of the back door. We were in a courtyard perhaps fifty yards square, cobbled and empty. The house itself formed one side of the square, and long farm buildings the other three sides. At the far end was the stable-block, two-storied like the house, and this is where he took us. We climbed up the open wooden stairs and into the long room. It was immaculately swept and clean, its short walls whitewashed with lime, the windows uncurtained. There was no light, but the clear moon streamed in and we could see easily.

"Here you are," said Mr. Devereux, his whole manner suddenly more relaxed and friendly. "You'll be comfortable here. Get off to sleep as soon as you can."

We heard him go down the stairs and pull the door behind him. The latch fell with a smooth click. Charlie Bond began to giggle.

"You certainly told him," he said to me. "You should have seen your face when you thought you weren't going to have any supper!"

"Why not?" said Del. "You'd have grumbled most if we had come to bed with empty stomachs."

There were hand basins at the far end of the room and we washed in the cold water, unrolled our sleeping bags, and threw them on three beds near one of the windows. We turned in fairly soon. Normally we would have talked together for an hour, but we didn't say much that night and everything grew still. I don't know whether Charlie and Del slept, but I certainly didn't. I was happy and warm there, and I began to think of Charlie walking down the darkening cloisters of the abbey, his voice echoing along the roofless walls. I saw once again the regular turning of Del's legs and feet as he pedalled along in front of me on the road to

Abergavenny, monotonously around and around. I expect I was going to sleep.

What brought me to my feet was startling enough. A door opened in the courtyard, then there was a confused clatter of feet. That was all right. It was the scream that stretched me. Not a scream of fright, but a high-pitched, whinnying scream, rather like that of a horse. And then there was a regular, light, galloping sound on the cobbles below. I was at the window at once, Del and Charlie looking over my shoulders.

The moonlight had divided the courtyard into almost exact halves, the area near us being brilliantly lit, that against the house in deep shadow. Mr. and Mrs. Devereux stood in the full moonlight, close together, almost in the center of the yard. Mr. Devereux had a rope in his hands. It reached into the shadow, and Mr. Devereux and his wife turned slowly, facing the galloping as it raced through the darkness. We did not know what to expect.

Out into the moonlight, roped about his waist, raced a boy of our own age, his arms thrashing the air, his unkempt pale hair bouncing on his head. Round and round he went, his heavy boots thumping and sparking on the cobbles, in and out of the revealing light. His face as he raced towards us was empty, an idiot's face; froth was forming around his mouth. Every time he raced into the dark, he screamed his shaken cry.

After a while, Devereux pulled in the rope, taking the boy in his arms. Now that he was still, we could see that the boy was unbelievably bent and frail. He could not walk properly, but that may have been from exhaustion. They went, all three, into the house, closing the door so softly that we could not hear it at all.

Del and Charlie were sitting on their beds, their faces turned towards the window, appalled and horrified. I don't know what we said to each other, or indeed if we said anything at all at that time.

That was thirty years ago. On holiday last year, driving

aimlessly in the region, I came across the valley once again. I didn't recognize it at first. The road was wider and better surfaced, and there was an air of prosperity about the place. But the abbey was the same. There were many visitors there, and I walked along the grass, remembering Charlie Bond who was killed in Africa in 1942 and Del Wellington who lives somewhere near Manchester and is a chemist.

I drove on, up the hill. The Youth Hostel is still there, still a hostel. It was a warm day, full of summer, but momentarily all I saw were the lucid moonlight and the faces of my two friends, as clear as my hand; all I heard was a ragged galloping over the cobbles.

Away Away in China

Early rising had always been a pleasure for him. Even when he had been in control of great industrial complexes, the prosperity of cities dependent on his judgment, able to order his life into whatever patterns he chose, he had still been at his office at eight every morning. Now, five years retired, the habit was part of him. He enjoyed the young day as much as he had when a boy.

He got up this morning very early. He had set his alarm clock the night before knowing he would not need it, and now, ten minutes before its stridency was ordered, smugly he turned it off. He shuffled his feet into decorous slippers, put on his robe, and went briskly to the bathroom. He shaved with small, precise movements and then took a shower. When he came out he was glowing. His table was prepared and he stood checking it, item by item, admiring his silver, his white tablecloth. Taking a can of orange juice from the refrigerator, he poured some into a tumbler and drank it slowly, waiting for the kettle to boil. The glass turned pearly in his hand and his teeth ached momentarily from the cold of the orange juice. He ate a piece of toast, unhurriedly, savoring it, and drank a cup of tea without milk. Afterwards he washed the dishes and put them away. It was by choice he lived alone. He walked into the bedroom and, as neatly as if he were packing a parcel, folded the sheets to the foot of the bed. Mrs. Smethurst would come in and make all ready for his return. Really, he had no need to employ her. Orderly and careful, he made no untidiness, was meticulous in all he did, evidence of his good taste and unostentatious money was everywhere. Yes, he was wealthy and he lived comparatively simply; that's all there was to it. He was never lonely; a man of resource was not lonely.

Clothes were important to him and he chose them seriously. They were expensive, muted, very elegant. Today he would wear a cream shirt, silk, new, tactfully cut, with a Paisley bow tie. His suit, which he had put out the evening before, was Donegal tweed, least heavy of all tweeds, and he was tall and slim enough to carry it. He remembered how carefully he had chosen the material three years before, and that he had paid enough for the suit to fit him perfectly. The cloth was subtly woven, in its mix was a hint of pink; never obtrusive, it was confident, somehow, and healthy. His shoes were hand-made and lovingly polished, but not new. When travelling he always saw to it his feet were comfortable. He stood in front of the mirror and recognized his vanity. He was as lean and straight as he had been long ago when he set out from his village, the newly qualified accountant, to that job in the Midlands. Puffing his lips in contempt, he thought of the ugly cheap suit he had worn then, thought of the dirty room in which he had been forced to work, in that gimcrack engineering firm. Well, it hadn't lasted long, he had soon moved to better things. He looked fine, his theatrical white hair brushed back, his face untroubled. As he straightened his shoulders more firmly he heard the newspaper fall through the letter-box.

He opened the door, the paper in his hand. It was dark, but little waking sounds of daylight came to him, the smell of the garden. Stars in the sky were bright as frost and it was going to be a clear day. Raincoat and case were ready for him in the front hall and he put his paper with them, on top of the case, near the neat label with his name, Alan Gwyther.

The taxi came at seven-thirty. He had never learned to drive and looked upon that ability as an accomplishment of

unimportant people. He had been accustomed to travelling
in pampered cars, Daimlers, Bentleys, for the last twenty of
his working years a succession of immaculate limousines
from Rolls-Royce. Uniformed chauffeurs, shut away from
him by plate-glass shields, had driven him to hotel and
conference. He could not remember any of these men
clearly, although he recalled the name of the first of his
drivers: Thwaite, a Yorkshireman. Dead now, thought Alan
Gwyther, a long time dead. He had treated the men well,
asked about their families, thanked them fully when a journey was over, gave generous tips. It had paid him to do so.
Thwaite's face, long and pale, came unbidden to him, and
he heard again his flat Yorkshire voice. The man had been
ashamed of his accent; he had sent his daughter to elocu-
tion lessons despite Gwyther's sturdy opinion that an able
child would learn how to speak properly once the need became obvious.

"Good morning, good morning," he said heartily to the
taxi driver. "Good of you to come so promptly."

They took thirty minutes to reach the station and
Gwyther waited another ten before his train pulled in.
He travelled first class, in a reserved seat, and a young por-
ter, still slack with sleep, carried his case and saw him to
his compartment. He was alone. He sat straight-backed in
his corner seat, the folded newspaper on his knees, his
competent hands relaxed. In Wales, he thought, they'll be
having their breakfast, my sister and her husband and her
daughter. Soon they'll be bustling around in case some tiny
aspect of my welcome has been overlooked. The whole village will know I'm about to visit them—I shall come to them
like a missionary from another civilization. People will call
on flimsy pretexts just to catch a glimpse of me. He was
amused by his fancy. Well, he was eager enough to see
them.

The train gave a series of little coughs and barks and
began without hurry to leave the station. On the road below
the railway bridge he could see files of men cycling to work.

It was bright daylight now, and a clear sun, too early for real heat, shone in the faces of the men, giving them unnaturally high colors. The slate roofs of the houses were more blue than the sky. Of course, he thought, these visits are good for me. They are necessary, they nourish me. They renew contact with my roots. He looked down at his impeccable suit and smiled.

Each time he made a visit to his sister's place he gave the suit he travelled in to his brother-in-law. Davy would accept the gift unwillingly, protesting, muttering. He could see Davy as he had been two years ago, holding the coat at arm's length, his eyes flickering doubtfully.

"Go on man, take it," he'd said. "Take it, Davy. You and I are of a size—I've too many suits. I can't wear them all." And this was true. He knew that a powerful agent of his slightly malicious generosity was his wish to see Davy so discomfited, so unable to deal with the situation. He suspected that each of his given suits had been examined, assessed, admired, and put away in the wardrobe never to be worn. Poor Davy, he thought, and his stiff-backed, stumbling pride. He leaned back in content. He was cultured and assured, with the mellow confidence of long and recognized success. He had been in charge of great affairs and even now was not without power. The train, gathering momentum, hurled itself south through brightening England. It was going to be a hot day.

Urgent, obsessed by the demands of its time-table, the train sped through the bleak West Riding towns he knew so well. By lunch time they were running west through the Midlands; on his way to the dining car he spent five minutes looking with distaste at the bulbous chimneys of the potteries, imagining what his life would have been had he stayed there.

I'm well out of it, he thought, and then with a little sharp surprise, I've been very lucky.

Although the food was indifferent, the vegetables limp and yellow and the meat stringy, he lingered over his meal.

The half bottle of claret was thin and metallic, but he enjoyed it, sensing the faint pink it brought to his cheeks. There would be no wine at his sister's house. He paid his bill and made his way along the swaying train to his compartment. They were passing through civilized Worcestershire countryside, heavy with harvest; heat haze trembled at the far edges of fields. Reaching his seat, he found a young woman sitting opposite. She must have got on at Kidderminster or Worcester. They smiled at each other, saying nothing, and he settled, picked up his newspaper, looked at her.

She was much the age of his niece, perhaps thirty. He liked her hair, dark as Mary's, and she looked like Mary, too. She was dressed in a summer-weight costume of pale fawn, the jacket of which was thrown over an empty seat. Her blouse was plain and expensive, her shoes excellent. She sat coolly groomed, her hands in her lap, relaxed and composed under his gaze. He approved of her. He thought again how much he looked forward to seeing Mary. A stubborn girl though, a mind of her own, that one. She should have left home years ago—with her ability he could have helped her to something worthwhile, she would have climbed. But she wouldn't leave. The hot afternoon entered the carriage and the old man sat deliberately upright against the heavy somnolence of the journey. Outside, the stubble glittered in the sun, the rich fields patched by shadows under the trees, the top-heavy elms and the wide oaks. He would have spoken if silence had not been so easy, if the warm steady rocking of the train had not lulled him into a state of paradoxically watchful sleep, if the golden and perfect fields had not come towards him one after the other, like an endless, beautiful country of his imagining.

In one of the fields, in a corner almost immediately below the raised embankment, a shot of color held his eye. Two birds fed there in cautious harmony. One, its mail of feathers polished hard in the yellow light, a small, Oriental monarch strutting, like fine silk glittering, one was a pheasant. One leg uplifted and paused in a high step, thin claws stretched towards the ground, there it stood, neck stretched to peck at the stems. The other, humbler because of its shorter legs and small size, was a fantail pigeon, flown from a dovecote to glean in the cut fields. The spun metal of the pheasant and the blazing white of the dove burned against his gaze. As he leaned forward, not wanting to miss an instant of vision, the pigeon flapped puffily a yard into the air, landing again as untidily as a handkerchief. It was unimaginably white against the brown stalks of felled wheat and the deeper bronze of the pheasant. He gaped momentarily at the heraldic birds. Then they were gone and he was left, one hand against the glass of the window, half pointing, expressing both his own delight and loss and the hope that the girl too had seen the marvel.

She nodded at him. He could see she was amused, and his answering grin was shamefaced, recognizing his comic transformation from drowsing old man.

"I've always been fascinated by birds," he said. "It's always astonished me that they should exist in the same world as us. There's a sense in which I understand animals, they are akin to us, have solid bones like us; but birds are so alien, so foreign. . . . When I was a boy in the country I would hold young birds from the hedgerow nests in my hands, and know absolutely that my palms did not understand what it was they held. Those extraordinary feathers—well, you saw the pheasant."

She looked at him gravely.

"I've not thought about it," she said. "Birds fly across the sky and I see them, but I don't recognize them although I like the patterns they make. I am not concerned about them."

This seemed to him astonishing. Everything that came to his eyes he classified, recognized, in a sense acquired.

"Are you travelling to Wales?" he asked.

"Yes," she said. "My parents have retired there, at Swansea, and I shall join them for a brief time."

The girl talked easily. She was interesting and amusing and he enjoyed the journey enormously. They left the train at Swansea, she to meet her parents and he to travel in the single Pullman carriage that went on into Pembrokeshire. They shook hands like old friends.

"You may not see anything as dramatic as your two birds," she said, "but you'll like Wales. After a week you'll not want to leave."

He shook his head, thinking of his books, his music, his house. Already they seemed too far away. But he was pleased the girl had not recognized him as Welsh, that he had not been betrayed by his speech. Long ago he had tamed his accent until it was formidably neutral, restrained the modulations of his voice until it was cool and objective. The Pullman filled up with young soldiers returning noisily to Ireland. They piled their rough equipment where they could; unbearably red and moist in their coarse uniforms, they lounged awkwardly, their strong legs thrust before them. It was suddenly very hot in the carriage. Hunched in his seat, he was unreasonably irritated and uncomfortable. He was tired. The journey was far too long. He hoped Mary would have a car to meet him at Carmarthen.

Mary was waiting for him on the platform, waving like a child, yet she saddened him. He had not expected her to look so old, so visibly defeated. He climbed from the train quietened by her watchful eyes, the lines of tiredness and disappointment on her face. Her clothes were drab and ordinary, there was nothing left of her old vivacity. She held in one hand a bag of heavy groceries, and the knuckles stood out raw and bony as a man's. He saw to his distress that she was not like the fashionable girl in the train; she was clumsier, older, beaten.

"Uncle Alan," she said. "Lovely to see you. Did you have a good journey?"

"Fairly," he said, "fairly good. Perfect as far as Swansea, but after that . . ." He held up a hand in dismissal. "How's your mother?" he asked.

"Waiting to see you, of course," said Mary. "This is Mansel, Mansel Edwards from the village. You don't know him. He had some business in town this afternoon and he's waited to drive us home."

A serious young man stepped forward. He wore jeans and a faded blue shirt, the sleeves rolled. His arms and face were weathered and his supple boots covered with fine summer dust. He was inches shorter than Gwyther. He nodded, picked up the case without effort, and led the way to the car.

"Sit in front, Mr. Gwyther," said Mansel. "It's cooler."

Windows open for the buzzing heat, they moved through the town and into the hills. He knew every inch of this road. Twice a day he had travelled it when serving his articles with Phineas Griffiths; around the next bend would be The Rock and Fountain, the inn where he had met his friends on Saturday evenings; above the quarry was the farm where Charlie Phillips had lived. Blindfolded he could have recognized every bend and dip in the way, known the different sounds of the accompanying river, by the total familiarity of it, by instinct; he could describe stone by stone each of the plain old houses that stood, lonely and arbitrary, at the roadside. Some, he saw, were empty and abandoned; insidious weather was picking them loose.

"Elizabeth Winstone's house," he said, pointing. "Who lives there now?"

"Nobody," said Mary. "She's dead, dead these two years."

"Elizabeth Winstone dead?" He was appalled. "She can't be. Why, it's not long since I heard her sing at a concert in York. Beautiful, a beautiful singer, a lovely voice."

He turned restlessly in his seat, shifting his hot old body to other comfortless positions. He was obscurely indignant at news of the singer's death, affronted and upset. He thought of her as he had seen her at York, vigorous, confident, her sturdy peasant's body controlled to the service of that gorgeous voice. Note after perfect note floated generously into his memory. Well, yes, it would have been six years ago.

"What happened to her?" he asked. His voice sounded querulous to him.

"Don't know," said Mary. She was looking back at the singer's house. "She returned from London, didn't like living there. And then one day we heard she was dead. It was in the papers; it's strange you didn't read it."

"I didn't read it," said the old man heavily.

"Not everyone can stand leaving home," Mansel said, not taking his eyes off the road. "Not everyone can take it, living far away."

His voice was so slow and thoughtful that the old man searched for some deeper meaning.

"You have to go," he said, "where your gifts and your energies take you. One place is much like another. You make the place in which you live, it becomes your creation. And it doesn't matter where you die."

"Not so." Mansel shook his head in gentle dissent. "Some people live more easily with their failure than others."

"Failure?" said the old man wonderingly. "But success was what Elizabeth Winstone had to live with. She had merely to organize her life about her achievement. She was brilliantly successful."

"Doesn't one kind of success imply a balancing failure?" asked Mansel. "Isn't it possible that her achievement was the result of a decision that was wrong for her, that it meant, for example, a life lived in places where she was unhappy?"

The old man grunted, but did not reply. He had taken his chances, followed his abilities where they led; but there was always an element of choice. Mansel would find out. He sat in silence until the car left the highway and turned down the narrower road to his sister's house. She stood outside her door waiting, wiping her hands on her apron, her dog at her side. Mansel drove away, his brown arm waving.

Gwyther was always surprised by his sister's frailness. In his mind she was the big girl on whom he had relied for almost everything. She had taken him to school on his first morning and on every reluctant morning until he was old enough to go alone; she it was who had so often bribed him from moods of stubborn temper with wild tales which set him laughing despite himself, his back still turned to her, had fed him ambitiously when their parents were out at market or sale, protected him equally from the assaults of older boys and the just punishments their father, that meek man, had sometimes threatened. He put his hands on her shoulders and they smiled at each other. The little shadows of his journey cleared away in the simple return of love.

"Margaret," he said, "you never change."

Over tea he was excited and talkative, remembering events he had thought long dead. He was very happy, laughing, eating more than he should. When Davy came in from his few fields he stood there unnoticed, listening to them laugh.

"You're here then, Alan," said Davy.

He was never easy with Gwyther. He thought of him as he had been as a boy, too quick of tongue and wit, thin, urgent, apart from the rest of them.

"Yes, I'm here," sang the dapper old man gaily. "Home is the sailor, Davy, home from the sea, and the hunter is home from the hills. Old times, old days—that's what we're talking about. Pull up your chair and tell me all your news."

There was nothing Davy could tell Alan Gwyther, he could think of nothing to interest him. All he could speak of were the slow, important changes of the seasons and the rituals of life and death. He thought hard.

"Oh, no news," he said. "The place is changing slowly, I suppose, all the older people going one by one—there are few left who remember you now, Alan. That's about all. And Glanafon Farm has been sold. To a Pole; nice man, I met him yesterday. Name of Poniatowski, but he speaks good English. So he should—he's been living here fifteen years, he told me."

"Language is a strange thing," said Margaret. "Look how well Alan speaks English, although he was brought up in the Welsh."

"Uncle Alan has forgotten his Welsh," Mary said. She had been quiet for so long that her voice, waspish and hard, startled them. She stared at her uncle. "He's completely English now," she said. "He looks English, he sounds English, his attitudes are English. He hadn't heard of Elizabeth Winstone's death."

He was dismayed by the unexpectedness and irrelevance of the attack, all his laughter collapsing about him. He got up quietly and took his bag up the stone stairs, each one worn thin and concave at the lip. He could remember his mother climbing these stairs, slowly, with such difficulty. That was long ago. He went into his room and put the case on the floor. Well, Mary must be a sad girl. All that ability and no opportunity to use it, her life without interest or variety, wasting her aimless time on trivial affairs. She had been such a bright little thing. And not married of course. Perhaps that had left her saddened and disappointed. He sat on the bed and looked out of the window. The field sloped steeply down, interrupted by an untidy summer hedge, the long whips of its brambles waving, to the stream that ran alongside the village street. He could look right on to the rooftops, identify the houses, people them with the families who had lived there sixty years before. He had known them all, every one of them. The short grass of the hills was a brilliant, moist green, except for three or four fields where late hay stood uncut. Davy's field was like a lawn, cropped tight by sheep and his short-tempered Michaelmas geese. When he heard a car stop outside the door he went downstairs. It could have been someone he knew, a friend from the old days come to see him; but it was only Mansel and his wife.

Mansel's wife was a teacher. A fair, plump girl, she sat in a fireside chair talking of the children in her class. She was so lively, so droll a mimic that the old man's spirits rose.

"And do you teach them everything?" he asked. "You must be wonderfully busy."

"They're only seven and eight years old," she said, "so there's nothing brilliantly academic about it. I cope quite well with everything except music, and then I'm hopeless."

Mansel was looking at her with amusement.

"No false modesty," he said. "You may not be the world's best pianist, but you're not bad. In any case it's a lot easier than teaching those little kids in Malaya."

He turned to Alan.

"When we were out there," he said, "in the Far East, she used to have a class under the trees in the center of the village. She didn't understand the language at first, but they got on very well together, she and the little brown kids."

"How I envy you," said the old man, "going out to Malaya. Europe I know well, of course, and I've made many business trips to America and Canada, but never to the East. I could have gone, but I was always too busy."

"Alan is a great traveller," said his sister. "Where was it you were last year, Alan? Salzburg, wasn't it?"

"Mansel is a forester," said Mary, "and he's been everywhere."

"Hardly everywhere," Mansel said, "but we've tried to go wherever the big forests are. We went out East the day after our wedding and we were there three years. We've been to Africa too, and we spent some time in Canada and in South America."

"Now we're home," said his wife, "looking after Welsh forests and Welsh children. But we've been all over the world."

Amused and attracted as he was by the girl's cheerful

candor, her uncomplicated good humor, Gwyther was nevertheless piqued. He was a competitive man, a winner. Always in this house he had been the one to relate tales of travel and adventure, and now he was outfaced by a pair of youngsters.

"What about the songs?" he called. "What songs did you teach the little Malaysians? What songs did we learn as children, Margaret?"

"The song you always sang, and you sang it until we were sick of the sound of it," his sister said, "was 'Draw, Draw yn China.' I can remember Father threatening to send him to China if Alan sang it once more, just once more."

"Of course," said Gwyther, laughing. "Of course."

He began to sing quietly, the tune suddenly as familiar as his skin, and then stopped in consternation.

"You're right, Mary," he said. "I have forgotten a lot."

But Mary sang alongside him, bringing the words back to him. He stumbled after her, his eyes on her mouth to catch the first syllables of words that he had lost.

"Draw draw yn China a thiroedd Japan,"

they sang together.

"Plant bach melynion s'yn byw,
Dim ond eilunod o'u gylch ym mhob man,
Neb i ddweud am Dduw."

Confident now, he swung into the last lines.

"Iesu, cofia'r plant,
Iesu, cofia'r plant,
Anfon genhadon ymhell dros y môr,
Iesu, cofia'r plant."

The laughter and clapping elated Gwyther. He caught Mary's hand.

"To the parlor," he cried, "all of us, we'll all sing it together."

He sat down at the old American organ, pushing away at the pedals. It hadn't been used for years and he worked hard, the wooden treadles clacking and grumbling before the dry bellows held enough air to carry a tune. Only Mary had come with him, and along the passage he could see a shaft of electric light come from the kitchen. He could hear Mansel's voice talking quietly and Davy's deep monosyllabic answers. He began to play, his stiff fingers accurate on the naïve melody. He and Mary sang together. She stood beside his chair, singing seriously, her hands clasped in front of her like a little girl. Well, she was loyal, this one. When they had finished he closed the organ. It had been his father's. They left the room and went back to the lit kitchen. The quiet talking went on around them. It was as if nobody had heard him sing.

Later, in his room, the day's invisible humiliations came sourly to him. The night was cool; it was like the death of summer. His sister had turned back his sheets and the blanket carried near the top two wide bands of color. It was new, a thick blanket of traditional design, woven locally. There had been one exactly like it on his bed when he had been a child. Many nights when he had been small he had lain in the dark, feeling the texture of the blanket as delicately as he could, with his fingertips. He had been convinced that he could tell the difference in the color of the wool by feel, that when he reached the pink band, or the green one, he would know by subtle difference of the wool. The moment he thought his hand had decided another color he would use his torch, a flat torch with an imitation leather case and three glass lenses, one red, one white, one green. But this was a new blanket. He switched off his light and sat on the bed. It was incredible that he could have forgotten the words of that old hymn. How foolish he had been to imagine that they would all troop into the parlor to sing with him. He began to whisper the words of the song to himself and then, obstinately, turned them to English in his mouth.

"Away away in China and the lands of Japan
Little yellow children live.
Nothing but idols around them everywhere . . ."

He sat on his white bed and looked out into the night. He was away in China all right. Grimly he remembered the pheasant and flawless dove he had seen that afternoon, taking what comfort he could from the memory. He thought of his house, lonely and cold and deserted as he was, distant now as the idea of safety. He got stiffly into bed, sliding his thin legs along the sheets. He had forgotten to bring a glass of water. He would do without. A burst of men's voices came up from the village as the inn closed its doors after the evening's pleasure. He would not have been able to recognize one voice had he been there, not one voice. Perhaps he had been at the center of things too long, perhaps his place was in the shadowy margins. The geese cackled briefly from the melancholy field below his window. He lay still and straight in the bed as a scatter of unexpected rain hit the pane, irregular, hard, stinging like tears.

꧁ A Roman Spring

I have this place in Wales, a small house set in four acres of pasture, facing north. It's simple country, slow-moving. I look down my fields and over a narrow valley, green even in winter. I go whenever I can, mainly for the fishing, which is splendid, but also because I like to walk over the grass, slowly, with nobody else about. The place is so silent that you discover small noises you thought had vanished from the world, the taffeta rustle of frail twigs in a breeze, curlews bubbling a long way up.

It's astonishing the old skills I find myself master of when I'm there, satisfying things like clearing out the well until its sand is unspotted by any trace of rotten leaf and its water comes freely through in minute, heavy fountains; or splitting hardwood with a short blow of the cleaver exactly to the point of breaking. I've bought all the traditional tools, the rasp, the band saw, the edged hook, the long-handled, heart-shaped spade for ditching. After a few days there I adopt an entirely different rhythm and routine from my normal way of living. Nothing seems without its purpose, somehow. I pick up sticks for kindling as I walk the lanes; I keep an eye cocked for changes of the weather.

We went down in April, my wife and I, for the opening of the salmon-fishing season. The weather had been so dry that the river was low, and few fish had come up from the estuary, ten miles away. I didn't care. We had a few days of very cold wind, and I spent my time cleaning the hedges of old wood, cutting out some wayward branches, storing the sawn pieces in the shed. After this I borrowed a chain saw from my neighbor Denzil Davies, and ripped through a couple of useless old apple trees that stood dry and barren in the garden. In no time they were reduced to a pile of neat, odorous logs.

They made marvellous burning. Every night for almost a week I banked my evening fires high with sweet wood, and we'd sit there in the leaping dark, in the low house, until it was time for supper. Then, one morning, the spring came.

I swear I felt it coming. I was out in front of the house when I felt a different air from the south, meek as milk, warm. It filled the fields from hedge to hedge as if they had been the waiting beds of dry ponds. Suddenly everything was newer; gold entered the morning colors. It was a Sunday morning. I walked through the fields noticing for the first time how much growth the grass had made. From some neighboring farm, perhaps Ty Gwyn on the hillside, perhaps Penwern lower down the valley, the sound of someone working with stone came floating through the air. I stood listening to the flawless sound as it moved without a tremor, visibly almost, toward me. "Chink," it came, and again, "chink," as the hammer chipped the flinty stone. I turned back to the house and told my wife. We had lunch in the garden, and afterward we found a clump of white violets as round and plump as a cushion, right at the side of the road. They grew beside a tumbledown cottage which is also mine, at the edge of my field where it meets the lane. The cottage is called Hebron. It wasn't so bad when I bought the place—I could have saved it then, had I the money—but the rain has got into it now, and every winter brings it closer to the ground. It had only two rooms, yet whole families were raised there, I've been told. We picked two violets, just as tokens, as emblems of the new spring, and walked on down the hill. Ruined and empty though it is, I like Hebron. I was pleased that the flowers grew outside its door. As we walked along, a blue van passed us, and we stood in the hedge to let it through. Our lane is so narrow that very few people use it—the four families who live there, and a few tradesmen. But we didn't recognize the van. We heard the driver change down to second gear as he swung through the bend and into the steep of the hill, outside the broken cottage. We had a splendid day. In the afternoon we took the car out and climbed over the Preseli Hills to Amroth, in Pembrokeshire. The sands were empty; the pale sea was fastidiously calm. It was late when we got back.

The next day was every bit as perfect. I got up in the warm first light, made some tea, cleaned the ash from the grate, and went into the field. I took a small ax with me, so that I could break up a fallen branch of sycamore that lay beneath its parent in the bottom field. Beads of dew, each holding its brilliant particle of reflected sun, hung on the grass blades. I pottered about, smiling, feeling the comfortable heat between my shoulder blades. Over the sagging roof of Hebron I could see the purple hills of Cardiganshire rising fold on fold into the heart of Wales. I listened idly to my neighbor, whoever he was, begin his work again, the clink of his hammer on the stone sounding so near to me. It took me a little while to realize that it *was* close at hand. I was unwilling to believe that anyone could be away from his own house on so serene and beautiful an early morning. But someone was. Someone was chipping away inside the walls of Hebron.

I ran through the wet grass, reached the cottage, and looked through a gap where the stones had fallen out of the back wall. I could see right through to the lane. The blue van was parked there, and a thin, blond girl stood beside it, her long face turned down a little, her hair over her shoulders. The wall was too high for me to see anyone in the house.

"What goes on?" I said. I couldn't believe that my ruin was being taken away piecemeal. The girl didn't move. It was as if she hadn't heard me.

"Who's there?" I called. "What do you think you're doing?"

A young man stood up inside the house, his head appearing opposite mine through the hole in the wall. He was dark, round-faced, wore one of those fashionable Mexican moustaches. He had evidently been kneeling on the floor.

"Just getting a few bricks," he said, his face at once alarmed and ingratiating. He waited, smiling at me.

"You can't," I said. "It's mine. The whole thing is mine— cottage, fields, the lot."

The young man looked shocked.

"I'm sorry," he said. "I've had permission from the local Council to take stuff away . . . They say it doesn't belong to anyone . . . I'm sorry."

"The Council are wrong," I said. "This cottage belongs to me."

I felt stupid, standing there, talking through a ragged gap in a wall three feet thick, but there was no way of getting around to him, except by walking back up the field, through a gate, and down the lane to the front of the house, where the white violets were. The thin, silent girl was standing almost on top of the flowers, which made me obscurely angry. I turned around and hurried off, alongside the hedge. As I went I heard the van start up, and Hebron was deserted when I got back. I opened the door. They'd taken the frames out of the windows, the wooden partition which had divided the little house into two rooms, and an old cupboard I had been storing there. I was incredulous, and then furious. I looked down at the floor. All my marvellous quarry tiles had been prized up and carried away. I could have wept. Nine inches square and an inch thick, the tiles had been locally made over a hundred years ago. They were a rich plum color, darker when you washed them, and there were little frosted imperfections in them that caught the light. They were very beautiful.

I ran up the road, calling for my wife. She came out and listened to me, her obvious sympathy a little flawed because she was also very amused. She had seen me stamping along, red-faced and muttering, waving aloft the hatchet I had forgotten I was holding.

"No wonder they vanished so quickly," said my wife. "You must have looked extraordinary, waving that tomahawk at them through a hole in the wall. Poor young things, they must have wondered what sort of people live here."

I could see that it was funny. I began to caper about on the grass in an impromptu war dance, and Denzil Davies came up in his new car. As far as Denzil is concerned, I'm an Englishman, and therefore eccentric. Unmoved, he watched me complete my dance.

But I was angry still. I could feel the unleashing of my temper as I told my story to Denzil. "They had a blue van," I said.

"It was a good market in Carmarthen last week," said Denzil carefully, looking at some distant prospect. "Milking cows fetched a very good price, very good."

"Took my window frames, my good tongue-and-groove partition," I mourned. "My lovely old cupboard."

"I believe the Evanses are thinking of moving," said Denzil. "Of course, that farm is getting too big for them, now that Fred has got married. It's a problem, yes it is."

"A young man with a moustache," I said. "And a girl with long, fair hair. Do you know them, Denzil?"

"I might buy one or two fields from old Tom Evans," Denzil replied. "He's got some nice fields near the top road."

"They stole my quarry tiles," I said. "Every bloody one."

Denzil looked at me with his guileless blue eyes. "You've never seen my Roman castle, have you?" he said. "Come over and see it now. It's not much of an old thing, but professors have come down from London to look at it. And one from Scotland." Kitty excused herself, saying she had some reading to catch up on. I sat beside Denzil in his new blue Ford, and we bumped along the half mile of track that leads to his farmhouse. I'd been there before, of course.

Denzil's farmyard is full of cats. After evening milking he always puts out an earthenware bowl holding gallons of warm milk. Cats arrive elegantly from all directions and drink at their sleek leisure.

We left the car in the yard, and climbed through the steep fields to a couple of poor acres at the top of the hill. Although high, the soil was obviously sour and wet. Clumps of stiff reeds grew everywhere, the unformed flowers of the meadowsweet were already recognizable, and little sinewy threads of vivid green marked the paths of the hidden streams. Right in the middle of the field was a circular rampart about four feet high, covered with grass and thistles, the enclosed center flat and raised rather higher than the surrounding land. I paced it right across, from wall to wall, and the diameter was nearly seventy feet. There was a gap of eight or nine feet in the west of the rampart, obviously a gateway. It was very impressive. Denzil stood watching me as I scrambled about. Everything I did amused him.

I took an old, rusty fencing stake to knock away the thistles growing on top of the bank and forced its pointed end into the thin soil. I didn't have to scratch down very deeply before I hit something hard, and soon I uncovered a smooth stone, almost spherical and perhaps two pounds in weight. I hauled it out and carried it down to Denzil. It was gray and dense, quite unlike the dark, flaky, local stone used for building my own cottage. And Hebron too, of course. I scored my thumbnail across it, but it didn't leave a scar. It was incredibly hard. Faint, slightly darker parallel lines ran closely through it, and a small irregular orange stain, like rust, marked its surface on one side. Denzil nodded. "That's it," he said. "That's what they made the walls with. Hundreds and hundreds of those round stones." My stone had been worn smooth and round in centuries of water, in the sea or in a great river. We were nine hundred feet high and miles from the sea or any river big enough to mold such stones in numbers, yet the Roman walls were made of them.

"They're under the road too," said Denzil. "The same stones."

I looked down from the walls of Denzil's castle. It was easy to see the road, now that he'd said it. A discernible track, fainter green than the land around, marched straight and true, westward from the Roman circle, until it met the hedge. Even there it had defied nearly two thousand years of husbandry. Generations of farmers, finding that little would grow above the stones, had left its surface untilled so that the road, covered with a thin scrub of tenacious blackthorn, went stubbornly on. We saw it reach the road two hundred feet lower down, halt momentarily, and then continue undeterred until it was out of sight. I knew it well, on the other side of the narrow road. It was the boundary of my fields. I had often wondered why I should have had so regular a strip of difficult and worthless shrubs.

"Just wide enough for two chariots to pass," said Denzil. "That's what one of those London men told me. But I don't know if he was right."

We looked with satisfaction at the straight path of the Romans.

"I've got new neighbors," Denzil said. "Down in Pengron. Funny people, come from Plymouth." He looked gently toward Pengron, a small holding invisible in its little valley. "They hadn't been here a week," he went on, "before they cut down one of my hedges. For firewood." He let his eyes turn cautiously in my direction. "Young fellow with a moustache," he said, "and a fair-haired girl."

"How interesting," I said, with heavy irony. "And do they have a blue van?"

"Strange you should ask that," said Denzil mildly. "I believe they do." We smiled at each other. "Can you see," Denzil said, "that the Roman road must have passed right alongside Hebron? There must have been a house on that spot for hundreds and hundreds of years, I bet." He was right. The old cottage sat firmly next to the dark accuracy of the traceable road, its position suddenly relevant. Carrying my stone, I walked back through the fields to have my lunch.

In the afternoon I drove over to Pengron. The house, its windows curtainless, seemed empty, but a caravan stood in the yard. The thin girl came to the door of the caravan, holding a blue plate in her hand. "Good afternoon," I said, but she didn't answer.

I've never seen anyone as embarrassed as the young man when he appeared behind her. He jumped out and hurried toward me. "I know," he said. "You want me to take everything back. I will, I'll take it all back this afternoon. I certainly will."

I felt very stiff and upright, listening to him. I could see all my tiles arranged in neat rows, six to a pile, on the ground. He must have taken over a hundred. He'd been at it for days, chipping away with his hammer while I wandered around in happy ignorance.

"I can understand," I said in the most stilted and careful manner, "that someone surprised in a situation as you were this morning is likely to say something, as an excuse, which may not be exactly true. But I have to know if you really have permission from the local Council to remove material from my cottage. If this is true, then I must go to their offices and get such permission withdrawn."

He was in agony, his face crimson with shame. I felt sorry for him as I stood unbendingly before him.

"No," he said. "No, I don't have any permission. It's just that someone up the village told me that he didn't think the old place belonged to anyone. I'll take everything back this afternoon."

I looked at my tongue-and-groove partition, my window frames. Unrecognizable almost, they formed a heap of firewood in one corner of the yard. Waving a hand at them in hopeless recognition of the situation, I said, "It's not much use taking that back, but the tiles, yes, and my cupboard, and anything else you haven't broken up." I walked back to the car, and he followed, nodding vehemently all the way. I was glad to leave him. When I looked in at Hebron later on, the tiles and the cupboard had been returned. I didn't enjoy myself much that day. It's stupid to be so possessive. The old cottage is an unprepossessing mess, not even picturesque. I ought to have been pleased that someone was finding it useful, but I wasn't. The lingering remnants of my anger pursued me through the night, and I was pretty tired next day. I took it easy.

I can't think why I went down to Hebron in the cool of the evening. I walked listlessly down the hill, becoming cheerful without energy when I found a wren's nest in the hedge. There never was such a place for wrens. They sing all day, shaking their absurd little bodies with urgent song. It was a good evening, cloudless and blue, a little cool air tempering the earlier warmth. I began to whistle. At quiet peace with myself, aimless and relaxed, I approached the cottage. When a man pushed his head and shoulders through the gaping window I was totally startled.

"How much for the house, then?" he said. He withdrew from the window, and stepping carefully, reappeared at the door, closing it slowly behind him. He was a very small man. Despite the mildness of the evening, he wore his reefer jacket wrapped well around him, and its collar high. He couldn't have been a couple of inches over five feet.

"It's not worth much," I said. He pushed his tweed cap off his forehead and smiled at me, a sweet, wise smile, but incredibly remote.

"No," he said, "not now. Oh, but it was lovely sixty years ago."

"Did you know it," I asked, "all that time ago?"

"Longer," he said. "More than sixty years ago. Since first I saw it, that is."

He stood outside the house, his hands deep in his pockets. He stood very carefully, protectively, as if he carried something exceedingly fragile inside him. His breathing was gentle and deliberate, a conscious act. It gave him a curious dignity.

"Know it?" he said. "For ten years I lived in this house. My brother, my mother, and me. We came here when I was five years old, after my father died, and I was fifteen when we left. I'm sixty-seven now." We turned together to walk down the hill. He moved slowly, economically. We had gone but a few yards when he stopped, bent down, and picked up a thin ashplant, newly cut from the hedge.

"I've been getting bean sticks," he explained. "I've left them along the lane where I cut them, so that I can pick them up as I go back."

We talked for a long time, and I warmed toward him. He was a great old man. We stood there, the evening darkening around us, and he told me of people who had lived along the lane in the days of his boyhood, of his work as a young man in the farms about us, of the idyllic time when he lived in Hebron with his mother and brother.

"But there's no water there," I said. "How did you manage for water?"

"I used to go up to your place," he said. "To your well. Times without number I've run up this road, a bucket in each hand, to get water from your well. We thought it was the best water in the world."

Slowly we moved a few yards on, and the old man lifted the last of his bean sticks from where it lay. Then he turned, faced resolutely forward, and prepared to make his way back to the village, perhaps a mile away over the fields.

"I've got to be careful," he said. "Take things very slowly, the doctor said. I'm very lucky to be alive." He placed his hand delicately on the lapel of his navy coat. "Big Ben has gone with me," he said. "Worn out. He doesn't tick as strongly as he used to." .

"Let me carry those sticks for you," I said, understanding now his deliberate slowness, his sweet tolerance, his otherworldliness. He was a man who had faced his own death closely, for a long time, and he spoke to me from the other side of knowledge I had yet to learn.

"I'll manage," he said. He bundled his sticks under one arm, opened the gate, and walked away. It was so dark that he had vanished against the black hedge while I could still hear his footsteps.

In the morning I went into the field below Hebron. It's not my field; Denzil rents it from an absentee landlord, and keeps a pony or two in it. There's a steep bank below the hedge, below the old Roman road, that is, and Hebron's garden is immediately above this bank. As I had hoped, the ground there was spongy and wet, green with sopping mosses. I climbed back up and into the garden, hacking and pushing through invading bramble and blackthorn, through overgrown gooseberry bushes. In the corner of the garden which overhangs Denzil's field, everything seemed to grow particularly well; the hedge grass was lush and rampant, the hazel bushes unusually tall. I took my hook and my saw, and cleared a patch of ground about two yards square. It took me most of the morning. Afterward I began to dig.

It was easier than I had expected, and I hadn't gone two spits down before I was in moist soil, pulling shaped spadesful of earth away with a suck, leaving little fillings of water behind each stroke of the blade. By lunchtime I'd uncovered a good head of water, and in the afternoon I shaped it and boxed it with stones from the old cottage, and while it cleared I built three steps down to it. It was a marvellous spring. It held about a foot of the purest, coldest water. I drank from it, ceremonially, and then I held my hand in it up to the wrist, feeling the chill spread into my forearm. Afterward I cleaned my spade meticulously until it shone, until it rang like a faint cymbal as I scrubbed its metal with a handful of couch grass. I knew that I would find water. For hundreds of years, since Roman times perhaps, a house had stood there: it had to have a spring.

I put my tools in the boot of the car and drove up to the village. If I meet my old friend, I thought, I'll tell him about my Roman spring. I saw him almost at once. He stood, upright and short, in front of the Harp Inn. There was nobody else in the whole village, it seemed. I blew the horn, and he raised both arms in greeting. I waved to him, but I didn't stop. Let him keep his own Hebron, I thought. Let him keep the days when he could run up the hill with two buckets for the best water in the world, his perfect heart strong in his boy's ribs. I had drunk from the spring, and perhaps the Romans had, but only the birds of the air, and the small beasts, fox, polecat, badger, would drink from it now. I imagined it turning green and foul as the earth filled it in, its cottage crumbling each year perceptibly nearer the earth.

I drove slowly back. The next day we packed our bags and travelled home, across Wales, half across England.

Percy Colclough and the Religious Girls

This is not my story at all. If not to Percy Colclough, then it belongs to my friend Tom Bevan, who told it to me in the taproom of an inn five miles out of Chichester on the A-286, the road to Midhurst, in Sussex. The name of the inn is the Horse and Groom, and it is about a hundred and fifty miles and thirty years away from the scene of the story Tom Bevan told me.

Tom had left school in 1935, when he was fourteen years old, and gone to work in the mines. Anyone could tell he'd once been a miner. He has the high, heavy shoulders that years of hacking and shovelling give to a man, particularly to one working in the South Wales pits, where there was never enough room to swing a pick properly. He also carries on his face a few of the thin, indelible-blue scars all miners wear.

He told me this story in his emphatic voice, his fanatical pale eyes fixed over my shoulder on the resurrection of his memories. I had never known Percy Colclough, but as soon as Tom Bevan began to speak I could see him plainly. He had started work on the same day, at the same age, and in the same Aberdare pit as Tom Bevan.

For four years they had worked near each other, Tom Bevan with his father and Percy Colclough with an older brother. Tom paraded before me the two young men, hard, spare, muscular. I saw them clearly; I knew the way their cheekbones shone after the ferocity of their evening shaves,

I could see the extravagant care with which they brushed their hair, docile with hair cream.

Work was brutal and hours were long in the mines in the late thirties. Together, Percy and Tom would walk over the mountain to the pithead, and they'd stumble home together after eight hours of backbreaking toil, too tired to speak, too tired almost to go to bed.

Their lives were extraordinarily narrow. From Monday morning until Friday night, they worked and ate and fell heavily to sleep, and all their pleasure would be packed into the brief weekend respite of Saturday and Sunday. Even this was an unadventurous leisure, almost ritualistic in its regularity: football, dancing, a visit to the cinema, drinking in the evening with one's friends. They never went farther from home than the dance hall at Pontypridd, eight miles down the valley. There they would gaze at young men from valleys four or five miles distant as if they came from the other end of the world.

Once a year, on a Saturday in August, they would go to Barry Island, or Porthcawl, or another South Wales coast town, in company with other miners, to a meeting of their trades union, the Miners' International Federation. I have a sepia image, as clear as if I myself had taken a photograph, of Tom and Percy, caught in midstep as they walk along the promenade, their white collars open, their jackets over their arms, the wide trousers then fashionable blown around their striding shins by a wind off the sea. That would have been a great journey for them—like a journey to Siberia, almost.

So it was enterprising of Tom when, on a Saturday morning in the cold spring of 1939, he walked breezily along to the railway station, its one platform empty in the pale-yellow sun, and bought a return ticket to Cardiff. Cardiff, twenty-four miles away, was the big city; in the evening, its lights warmed the sky with orange promises of the exotic as far north as Tom's village.

Tom went down on the nine-fifteen, walked like a famous

dandy around the two main streets, looked at the expensive shops and the girls newly blooming in the sun, had lunch in Woolworth's, went to a football match, and was home by seven-thirty. This was living. He told nobody of his escape from the valley, not even Percy Colclough. And the next Saturday he went to Swansea.

This was a longer journey and lacked the intoxicating, headlong directness of Tom's first venture. There was, for example, a change of trains at Neath, and he had to wait for ten minutes in a cold rain that drifted inexorably over the nearby hills and settled, as if forever, on the whole of Wales. Then his carriage was full of comfortable families going shopping. On his trip to Cardiff, Tom had had a compartment to himself, so that he could take two steps from window to window and miss nothing of the scenery on either side. He had sung loudly, in his resonant baritone, the popular songs of the day—"Begin the Beguine," "Blue Moon," "Stardust." But now he was forced to sit, silent in his steaming raincoat, between two plump women, pinned in by their elbows. He lost, gradually and hopelessly, the bold spirit of exploration with which he had begun the day.

He was depressed, and a little awed, by the iron magnitude of Swansea Station. As gray and wet as the rain outside, it glowered down at Tom, its metal noises ringing ominously through his head as he gave half of his ticket to the man at the gate.

Tom stepped cautiously out into the world. A huge square, as big as a village, stretched in front of him, its raucous traffic checked by an eloquent policeman on a dais. He was buffeted by people; the wind ripped at his slapping coat. It was all too much for Tom. He sidled along the pavement, his head down, searching for haven.

What he found was a small Italian café, squashed incongruously between the splendid buildings of more prosperous concerns. It was warmly shabby, its windows carried an array of advertisements for concerts and boxing matches, maroon paint peeled in strips from its door. With a sigh of relief, Tom stepped into its odorous darkness. A long counter stood along the far wall, the gleaming coffee machine, hissing to itself, at one end. Plates of sausage rolls, curling sandwiches, and doughnuts lay limply under glass covers. Behind the counter, a muttering, fat old man was just visible. You could order tea or coffee or Bovril or Horlick's. A little pot of crusted mustard stood on each of the four marble-topped tables. It was exactly like Carpanini's, in Aberdare. Tom was at home. He sat down in an upright and comfortless chair.

"I'll have a coffee," he said firmly, "if you don't mind."

"One coffee," said the fat old man. "Yes, sir."

"And a doughnut," said Tom.

"And a doughnut," said the old man. "Yes, sir."

The only customer in the safe dark of the café, Tom dozed away the remaining morning, his eyes half closed, like a cat. At one o'clock he took off his raincoat, hung it on a hook on the wall, and pondered over the menu the old man handed him. He liked its restraint and conservatism.

Pie and chips
Sausage and chips
Egg and bacon
Egg and chips
Sausage, egg, and chips
All with bread and butter and a cup of tea.

He read with approval.

"Sausage, egg, and chips," he said. "I like a good meal in the middle of the day."

"Yes, sir," said the old man. "Sausage, egg, and chips." He shuffled off to do the cooking.

Tom ate slowly, with conscious enjoyment. From time to time he glanced out the window, watching the rain stream down the glass through the advertisement for Typhoo Tea, seeing the hurrying wet figures of the passers-by. He was very happy. He wished only that he had a daily paper, and when the old man, without a word, brought him a grimy copy of the *Express*, he was pleased but not surprised. Propping it against the sugar bowl, he read placidly, sipping his tea like a young man with time to spare.

When the two girls came in, Tom lifted his cup to them in gentle courtesy and wished them a good afternoon. They were pink from hurrying, they shook out their wet coats with exclamations of relief and surprise, they smiled at Tom Bevan. One of them was tall, fair, and elegant. She moved like a colt.

"What a day," one of them said. "The usual, please, Algy."

"Egg and chips," said the old man. "Yes, Miss."

The girls sat two tables away from Tom Bevan, examining the contents of their parcels, chattering away as briskly as starlings. Tom looked at them with pleasure. He pushed away his paper and spoke to them.

"How do you girls like living in Swansea?" he said.

They stopped talking and considered.

"I've never lived anywhere else," said the tall, fair girl. "It's all right, though, living in Swansea. Very nice, really."

"I don't live in Swansea," the shorter, darker girl said. "I live in Dunvant, just outside. It's a village."

"We went to school together, didn't we, Elsie?" said the fair girl.

"And now we work together in an insurance office," said Elsie.

The old man came in, two plates held in front of him.

"Ooh! Thank you, Algy," said the girls together. "It looks lovely."

What nice girls, thought Tom Bevan, what pleasant manners. "I had sausage, egg, and chips," he said. "I believe in a good meal in the middle of the day."

"We've never had that," said Elsie, "although sometimes we have pie and chips. Mostly in the evening we have pie and chips, after the cinema. Don't we, Margaret?"

"That's right," Margaret replied. "In the evening." She looked up at Tom Bevan. "Where do you live?" she asked.

Tom Bevan told them. He told them about his journey to Cardiff; he told them of its glittering shops and its streets; he told them of the Taff River, black as oil, running through the heart of the town; he described the football match he'd seen. Then he told them of his work in the mine, and they listened carefully, interrupting him now and then with flattering little gasps of amazement.

"It's a world of its own, down there," he said. "I've seen things down there that would make you laugh, yes, and make you weep, too."

"You must have," said Margaret with admiration. "We don't know how you colliers stick it as you do. Now, our work isn't exciting at all."

"Not exciting," agreed Elsie, "but we have some fun, you know, in the office."

The girls looked at each other, smiling, their eyes shining.

They took Tom Bevan into the small universe of their office, described the manager, the clerks, the other typists, told him of the little practical jokes that enriched the passing days.

"That Mr. James can be a pig sometimes," said Elsie, "but he can't help it. He has asthma."

"There's nothing worse," confirmed Tom Bevan, "than a bad chest."

He held the palm of his hand for a moment on his own shirtfront.

"Do you know," he began, "that two winters ago, I had bronchitis so badly I couldn't breathe? I had to sleep all night sitting upright in an armchair, the blankets wrapped around me."

The girls, full of sympathy, nodded softly to him.

The afternoon sped by. Tom, preserving what he hoped would prove an interesting reserve, did not join the girls at their table, but he bought chocolate biscuits that they all three shared. He couldn't remember ever having met such attractive, sensible girls. He looked with satisfaction at their sophisticated clothes, their delicate shoes. There was no doubt that girls in the big towns knew how to behave.

When the girls got up to leave, Tom, springing to his feet to help them with their coats, felt keen disappointment. He handed them their parcels and moved to open the door for them.

"Good-bye," said Elsie. "It's been nice meeting you. I enjoyed our chat."

"Thank you," said Tom. "So did I."

"We might see you again," Margaret said. "We always have our lunch here on Saturdays."

"I'm often here myself," said Tom, with pardonable exaggeration. "I might see you next Saturday."

The girls stepped into the street, ducked their heads against the wind, and disappeared.

A glint of sun broke through the cluttered windows of the café. The rain had stopped. Tom took down his coat and shrugged himself into it. The world was warm and pleasurable. He said good-bye to the muttering old man, immobile behind the counter. "Nice little place you have here, Algy," said Tom. "Very nice little place."

The old man did not reply.

Outside, the streets had regained their normal proportions, the traffic was amiable and controlled. Tom strolled about for half an hour, returned to the station, caught a train, and departed for home. His carriage was empty, the late-afternoon light was golden, and Tom sang all the way to Aberdare.

On Sunday morning, Tom went to church, meeting, as he usually did, the tall and elegant figure of Percy Colclough. Percy was a deeply serious young man, and attended church three times every Sunday. He was astonished to

learn that Tom had been to Swansea, but, keeping the Sab-
bath for solemn matters, asked no questions.

The next morning, however, on the way to the pithead,
he spoke out boldly.

"What's it like in Swansea, Tom?" he asked.

"Lovely," said Tom. "Fine. They've got a huge station
and a very nice café there."

Percy Colclough laughed.

"It was raining," said Tom defensively, "and then I met
these two charming girls."

Percy Colclough stopped laughing. "Two charming
girls?" he said.

"Margaret and Elsie," confirmed Tom. "I'm meeting them
again next Saturday. You can come along if you like."

Percy whistled pensively. "I might," he said. "I just
might, at that."

All week long Percy found opportunities for nudging
Tom with an elbow, for winking slowly at him.

"Saturday," he'd say. "Still all right for Saturday, Tom?"

"I'll see you at the station about half past nine," Tom
would answer.

Tom was at the station early on Saturday. He had hurried
through the holiday streets, bright with strengthening
spring, but he knew that Percy Colclough would be there
before him. He bought his ticket, moved through the barrier, and walked on to the platform. Tall, slim, his dark suit
pressed and cleaned, Percy Colclough stood alone at the far
end of the platform. He turned his head but gave no other
sign of recognition. His black hat sat prim and straight on
his head.

Tom hurried up to him, noting with approval the details
of Percy's appearance—the glossy white shirt, the discreet
small flower in his lapel, the shoes polished like mirrors.
Under Percy's arm was a Bible.

"Good morning, Percy," said Tom, "and a lovely morning for our little escapade."

"Good morning, Tom," said Percy. "I think we may enjoy ourselves today."

Together the two young men stared down the track in the direction from which the train would come.

A heavy silence deepened until Tom could stand it no longer.

"For God's sake, Percy," he said hoarsely. "Why the Bible? Why the Bible, Percy?"

Percy Colclough stepped nearer. He looked with extreme care up and down the deserted platform. He lowered his voice, as if in fear that the heathen wind of April would lift his salacious words and scatter them broadcast over listening Aberdare.

"I was thinking," he said, like a convict, out of the side of his mouth. "Well, tomorrow being Sunday . . . and if these girls were any good . . . you know . . . we might stop over until tomorrow."

When Tom Bevan told me that, in the Horse and Groom, I couldn't stop laughing.

"And did you," I asked, "did you stop over?"

"No," said Tom Bevan. "Of course we didn't. Those were two very nice respectable girls. Went to church every Sunday, the same as we did."

Tom Bevan is a schoolteacher now. He lives in Hampshire, only a dozen miles from me. I rang him up to tell him I'd written this story, and he laughed.

"It's all true," he said. "Every word of it. And I'll tell you something else. Although he was so religious himself, when Percy Colclough found out that those two girls were also religious he was white with anger. He was angry for weeks, not speaking to me for over a month. And I never heard him say a good word about Swansea after that."